Vampire King
(Adult Fairy Tale, Cinderella Book 1)
By

Joanna Mazurkiewicz

Chapter One

Cindy, short for Cinderella, was walking around the market with her basket full of groceries while humming an old and well-known ballad to herself. She was hoping to be done with shopping soon enough and spend some time alone in town, before she had to head home. Shopping was the only time she had where she was able to escape the taunts and ridicule from her stepmother and annoying stepsisters who notoriously made her life difficult. There was also another reason why she enjoyed these weekly trips; Cindy hoped to finally see the forest ranger and find the courage to speak to him.

Cindy lived in the Farrington Kingdom that was ruled by the wealthy and powerful King Caspian II whom she had never seen with her own eyes, but apparently all the ladies in town were convinced he was incredibly good looking. Caspian also had a son a little older than Cindy, Prince Eric, who had been seen in town many times before.

She kept walking around, enjoying the weather with her basket already half full, knowing that she still had a little bit of time left on her hands. She kept wondering around between the stands, thinking about the day ahead, and enjoying being on her own. She spotted Charles, the forest ranger, by the meat stand. Her heart shuddered a little, and she tackled a lock of blond hair behind her ear, telling herself that she needed to be brave. This was her chance to approach him, hoping he would finally take notice of her.

Red Riding Hood, Cindy's former best friend, introduced Charles to Cindy a couple of years ago. Cindy was enchanted by him straight away, but soon after, he started going out with Red instead. As time went on, she developed a little crush on Charles, fighting her feelings, not wanting to hurt her best friend. Besides, Charles had never paid any attention to Cindy while Red was around before they started dating.

Deep down, Cinderella was feeling unsure about speaking to him at the market. What if he didn't want to talk to her? A few weeks ago, she heard that Charles had broken up with Red. Apparently, the two of them had a huge fight and went their separate ways.

Since Cindy and Red had a falling out, Cindy told herself that she didn't need to feel guilty anymore, but she worried that Red was still in love with him and Cindy wasn't sure if acting on her feelings would be appropriate.

She continued walking, lost in thought and when she was a meter away from Charles, someone pushed her from behind, causing her to drop the basket, falling face-first onto the ground at his feet. Vegetables scattered everywhere; embarrassed and wanting to leave right away, she tried to pick everything up as quickly as possible. When she went to grab a carrot, someone's hand landed on hers at the same time. Her heart leapt in her throat as she lifted her eyes, staring into Charles' intense, brown gaze that was only inches away from hers.

"Let me help you with that," he said, in a low voice that caused her insides to quiver instantly. Cindy was a little confused, because Charles was acting like he had no idea who she was.

"Thank you, Charles. I'm surprised to see you here alone today," she quickly said, trying to remind him that they actually knew each other.

"Sorry Cinderella, those barrels were a little too heavy and I lost my balance," said another voice. Cindy and Charles looked at Jack at the same time. The tavern owner was carrying three large wine barrels, looking a bit embarrassed about what had happened, as two other barrels rolled across the road.

"It's all fine young man, just be more careful next time," Charles said, sounding annoyed. Jack nodded, smiled at Cindy and then continued to walk towards the tavern, looking slightly baffled, probably because Charles had called him a young man. "Cinderella, what a pleasant surprise seeing you here."

"Oh stop it Charles, you know that I don't like being called Cinderella. Cindy is just fine," she chuckled, aware that she was already flustered and red. Charles helped her put her groceries back into the basket, then held her hand as he helped her to her feet. He smiled at her and Cindy felt a cold shiver crawl over her spine.

"Cindy, come walk with me. I'm browsing around the market today, and would love for us to catch up," Charles said, staring at her so intensely that she felt like she was going to lose her bearings again. Heat rushed to every part of her body.

"Sure, so are you buying something for Red? I haven't spoken to her in a while. I hope she's all right." Cindy asked, just to be sure that Charles and Red were no longer an item. She didn't want to feel guilty about flirting with him afterwards. Charles expression remained stilled. "I'm asking because I heard that you guys had a little disagreement."

"There's no other woman in my life, beautiful. Right now, all I want to know is where you've been hiding all this time?" he asked, when they stopped by the town fountain.

Cindy parted her lips, squeezing the handle of her basket, trying to deal with her racing pulse. Charles had never before called her beautiful, they had exchanged a few words here and there, but he seemed so different today. He was studying her face, noticing her for the first time and this made her feel special.

"I've been at home, you know doing my usual chores and helping my stepmother. Red and I haven't been seeing each other that much and I was concerned about her when people told me that you two had broken up," Cindy explained, feeling a little hot. She was also conscious of the time; she couldn't come home too late or she'd face her stepmother's wrath.

"Don't worry about Red, I'm sure she's already seeing someone else. I was wondering if you would want to spend some time with me today?" the forest ranger asked, moving a little closer and Cindy caught a wave of his cologne. It made her heart pound even faster and she told herself that Charles was acting a lot more mature than usual—and it was definitely good thing.

"Yes, I'm almost done with shopping and the weather is so nice today," she answered, feeling ecstatic that he wanted to keep her company.

Charles walked with her around the market, and they talked more than they ever had; Cindy could barely contain her excitement. He even bought her roses and kept asking her about her life with her stepmother and her stepsisters. Soon enough, Cindy had lost track of time, and quickly forgotten that she was supposed to head home over an hour ago. She always thought that Charles was only interested in his work in the forest, but after a few hours with him she realised that she had been wrong about him. He was well-read, travelled and she felt like they understood each other without words.

Charles ended up walking her halfway home. She wouldn't let him get too close just in case her stepmother was lurking about. When they were just about to say their goodbyes, he was already asking her when they could see each other again. At that moment, Cindy stopped being conflicted about her feelings. Charles had made it clear that his relationship with Red was over and he was ready to start fresh. Cindy even let him kiss her on the cheek. As she was walking away, he continued watching her from the distance and her heart was pounding away in her chest.

She couldn't believe her incredible fortune—Charles had finally noticed her and was interested. It was one of the happiest days of Cindy's life, because she was finally noticed by someone other than a drunken peasant. Everything was perfect until she arrived home, and her stepmother began shouting, asking her where she was all that time. Even through her stepmother's rant and threats, Cindy kept her radiant smile, knowing that soon enough she would see Charles again.

**

Cindy didn't have the opportunity to get out from under Ida's careful watch for a very long time after her meeting with Charles. Weeks went by and she eventually managed to see him in the forest while she was picking mushrooms. It was a short meeting and after an hour she had to rush back home, knowing that her stepmother would look for her if she was late again.

But tonight, she managed to sneak away unnoticed, and went straight to the local tavern, where Charles liked hanging out a lot. She was sitting alone, too afraid to take a sip of her wine or talk to anyone else. The forest ranger had been coming to the Fox Tail often and many people in town knew him. Cindy wasn't used to being out on her own, but she was missing Charles since they met in the forest a few days ago. He turned out to be a completely different man than she had originally thought.

With her, he was a gentleman, always asking about her passions, her stepmother and her dead father. She couldn't help but notice that over time she began developing real feelings for him.

Cindy sighed loudly, realising that her stepmother was most likely furious with her by now. Cindy left without her permission and went to town to meet a man that she'd had a serious crush on since as far back as she could remember. This kind of thing was unacceptable and simply wrong in high society. She was responsible and kind, not a troublemaker like her stepsisters. She always thought twice about everything she did, but tonight she decided to stop being compliant.

For the past few minutes she'd been telling herself that she needed to leave, otherwise the drunken peasant who'd been eyeing her boobs for a good ten minutes now would approach her instead. Besides, it looked like Charles wasn't coming after all, and Cindy didn't want to anger her stepmother even further. She left the house after dark to come to the tavern. It was a hell of an effort on her part, because normally she refused to go outside once the sun had gone down.

She began practising in her head what she wanted to say to him once he showed up and didn't even notice when someone approached her table. A split second later, goose pimples appeared on her arms and she lifted her head.

"Hello, my beautiful Cindy. I couldn't believe my eyes when I saw you tonight, sitting here all alone."

She didn't even need to look up or hear his voice to know that it was her Charles. He was now standing right in front of her. She thought that tonight he looked even more handsome than any other time that she had seen him. The only reason that Cindy snuck out tonight was because she truly missed him. On top of everything else, Cindy was done sitting around, waiting for her true love to appear out of thin air. She needed to take matters into her own hands.

Charles was very tall, with broad shoulders and dark, curly hair. Cindy remembered the way he stole a kiss the second time they met in the forest.

"Darling, you will be angry with me, but I can't seem to control myself around you," he told her a few weeks ago when they were lost in the forest, sitting on a broken tree. Cindy palms were damp with sweat and she felt warmth spreading throughout her body, causing her heart to pound loudly in her chest. When she looked at him to ask what he meant, he leaned over and captured her lips in his. Her mind screamed at her to react and before she could pull away, Charles brought her closer and continued kissing her deeply, devouring her completely.

She responded, and they kissed for ages. That night Cindy's body was on fire, but the squeaky noise of a bird from the nearest tree distracted her. She pulled away from Charles, telling him that she had to go, and ran back to the house. Since that night, Cindy couldn't stop thinking about the amazing kiss they shared together.

"I had to run some errands for my stepmother, and now I'm waiting here to pick up something from the shop later on," she replied, pulling away from her thoughts.

They hadn't seen each other since then and Cindy was going crazy being stuck at home. Everyone in town thought that Cindy was shy and innocent, because she was always so well behaved, but deep down she yearned to be more adventurous. She dreamed of having the whole fairy tale romance since she was a little girl. Over the past several years, she kept that dream deep inside her heart, thinking that soon someone special would appear and sweep her off of her feet. When her father was still alive, she often told him that one day she was going to marry a real prince, someone who would love her for who she was. Charles wasn't the prince that she'd always dreamed of, but he was a decent man. On top of that, Cindy thought that he was very attractive, kind and since he'd stopped seeing Red, he turned into a more decisive and interesting man. Besides, the only prince who lived in Farrington wasn't rushing into a marriage at all.

"Well, you don't have to be alone anymore my darling, because I'm here to keep you company. The past few days were torture and Sunday couldn't come soon enough, because I knew I would see you at the market again," he said, and sat down opposite her. For a split second, she could have sworn she saw his skin shimmer in the dim light of the tavern, but no. Her eyes must have misled her, because that was surely impossible. She knew him well enough by now.

After the kiss, they met a few more times at the market, but they never had much time to truly be with each other. After their first meeting in the market, Cindy's stepmother ordered her to do the shopping and come back home as soon as she was done. Ida must have noticed that Cindy came back looking happier than usual, and from that point on, she only gave her an hour to finish or she would have to suffer the consequences.

Her stepmother had been busy with paperwork all day and when she finally retired for the evening, Cindy slipped out through the back door. She didn't tell anyone where she was going. Her stepmother would never allow it, so Cindy wasn't ready to take any chances. She stood just outside of the door for at least half an hour, trying to dismiss her fear of the darkness before she forced herself to venture further. It wasn't fully dark at the time, the sun was slowly hiding behind the horizon, so it was easier for her to deal with her insecurities. She hadn't always been fearful of the dark, but something snapped inside her when her beloved father passed away several years ago—when she was only thirteen. Now every time she tried to go out during the night, her pulse started racing. She would suddenly be drenched with sweat and unable to breathe properly, so she started going out only in the daytime. Being out tonight was a feat in and of itself.

"Yes, I was counting the days, and couldn't stop thinking about you too," she admitted shyly. She also noticed that a few other women from town were shooting Charles flirtatious looks. They must have heard by now that he was single. Too bad he wasn't paying any attention to them.

He stared at her lips, and a warm buzzing sensation spread through her body. She felt excited about breaking the rules again. Before she bumped into Charles at the market, every day of her life was the same: she got up, cooked, prepared meals, fed the chickens, cleaned, then cooked dinner and by the evening she was so exhausted that she dropped dead on the bed, falling asleep instantly. Tonight she was actually doing something for herself.

Charles proved to her before that he was a wise man, but tonight Cindy was ready to move further and show him that she could truly commit to him. She didn't want to wait for the right moment, and felt that Charles was the man for her. The man that she could eventually marry.

She glanced out the window, seeing that it was already pitch black, and swallowed hard, sensing her growing anxiety. Fear was making her feel insecure and trivial, but she told herself to stay calm. Charles was there and he would walk her back to the house. She only had to ask.

"Cinderella … you're driving me insane, and I know that your stepmother is very strict, but I think you should introduce me to her. She would love me, and then we wouldn't have to sneak around anymore," Charles said, and accidentally or totally on purpose brushed his thighs against hers. She felt a jolt of electricity running down her legs, and suddenly realised that his face was only inches away from hers. She smelled his cologne, a fresh, musky scent that instantly turned her on.

"I don't know, maybe it's too soon. She would hate that I met with you in secret, behind her back," Cindy explained, remembering the past when she was standing at the window watching her stepsisters going out to parties, while she had to stay at home and clean.

It was disheartening and she knew that her stepmother hated seeing her happy. She was a little apprehensive about introducing the forest ranger to Ida.

"All right, my darling. In that case, let's get out of here right now, and walk around the forest for a bit. It's too crowded in here," Charles suggested, leaning even closer, and Cindy didn't have to think twice about it.

She had no idea what had gotten into her, especially considering her fear of the dark. But tonight she decided to become a new Cindy. She thought about her enchanting perfume and knew Charles would probably like it. She'd stolen it from her stepmother a few hours earlier, along with a very revealing white dress. Cindy wasn't the kind of girl to steal things, but her stepmother had taken most of her possessions when Cindy's father passed away. The dress used to belong to her mother, and she just knew it would look good on her. Besides, her stepmother wasn't a very nice person in general. Evil, to be exact.

"Yes, I would like that," she responded, and Charles smiled widely.

He stood up and reached out to take her hand. The forest ranger was only looking at her tonight, and after their secret meeting, Cindy was certain that he wanted her as much as she wanted him. Cindy needed to experience the touch of a real man. She'd been waiting for this kind of opportunity for far too long.

Ever since her father died, her life had never been the same. Her stepmother turned into someone completely different as soon as her father's will was read aloud. She became demanding, sharp, and started ordering Cindy around, making her clean and cook all day long. Apart from her stepmother,

Cindy had two stepsisters who were very cruel too her most of the time. She didn't like the way they called her names, and slapped her if she disagreed with them about something. Her stepsisters also had much more freedom than Cindy. It wasn't fair, but she knew that tonight her luck could finally change.

She had to find a man who would want to marry her so she could leave her stepmother and that horrid life behind forever.

"Come on my beauty, let's get out of here," Charles said, winking at her. In her head she was ready to give him her virtue. She was reeling with unbidden thoughts of things she'd never experienced before.

She took a few more sips of wine, giggled and then followed Charles outside the tavern. Her stepmother had never allowed her to drink, and right then Cindy felt a bit tipsy. Maybe the alcohol was making her a bit braver. At least it subdued her inhibitions and she wasn't afraid of going out into the night.

The tavern was located just outside the Fyrred Town, and her house was on the other side, near the river Cloud. The powerful King Caspian II was the owner of the entire land and he ruled the Farrington Kingdom fairly. Apparently, his wife passed away almost twenty years ago and he never married again.

"I wish that I could stop time somehow, I don't want to leave you later on," she told him when they were heading towards the forest. She was worried about her stepmother, but she needed to stand up to her once and for all.

Charles sighed loudly, like he understood where she was coming from. When he glanced at her, Cindy saw the lust in his eyes. She didn't even have to overthink this anymore. The forest ranger liked her, and Cindy was imagining him standing in front of Ida and asking for her hand.

They walked and talked for a bit. Most of the time Charles was asking questions about the stories that she liked reading and times spent with her father when he was alive. He always seemed very interested in her life.

An hour later, they were moving through the forest, laughing and chasing each other, trying to ease off the sexual tension. For a second, Cindy didn't care that it was so dark or that it would normally freak her out. None of it mattered at that particular moment, because she was finally alone with Charles.

He caught up with her after several minutes of playing around. He grabbed her from behind, while Cindy pretended to be scared. She screamed and they both fell to the ground. It took her several moments to realise that she was lying on top of him; her heart was jackhammering in her chest. She realised she was in a position she'd only dreamed of and didn't exactly know how to react—she had to wing it.

"You're so stunning, my Cinderella. I can't seem to control myself around you any longer. Where the hell have you been all my life?" he asked, staring at her with his intense brown eyes, practically undressing her with his gaze. Cindy's desire stirred in the pit of her stomach, and before she could think about a coherent response, Charles kissed her.

And oh boy that kiss made her toes curl, sending a stream of heat through her entire body. She didn't waste time, and instinctively grabbed Charles's cheeks and pulled him to her harder, then slipped her tongue into his mouth. Heat started ravaging her body as her nipples hardened. She wanted more.

They were twisting and turning on the cold ground, their bodies tangled with each other, and she loved every second of it. Suddenly Charles grabbed her arse, and started moving his hand underneath her dress. She didn't mind, she was turned on and wanted to stay with him forever.

"Oh yes, my sweet girl, you taste unbelievable," he whispered in her ear, touching the sensitive parts of her body that no one had ever touched before. Cindy arched her head backwards and gasped when Charles started sucking along the column of her neck, followed by feather soft kisses across her jaw until he reached her full mouth, while moving his long, thick fingers down her thigh once more.

She had never felt so liberated in her entire life, blood pounded in her ears and she instantly thought that he was the one.

"Cindy Rutherford, get off that man and out here right this instant or I'll drag you out from the bushes myself!"

The voice of her stepmother startled her and she jumped back to her feet like her arse was on fire. Blood rushed to her ears and she quickly glanced back at Charles, mortified. She had no idea how her stepmother had found her. They were in the middle of the forest, away from the road.

"I have to go," she muttered, thinking that her stepmother must have followed her all the way out there. It was the only logical explanation. She was just waiting for the right moment to embarrass her. Ida's sharp eyes were filled with fury, but Cindy wasn't really worried about how she might be punished.

She had interrupted her perfect date, making Cindy look like an idiot. Ida grabbed her elbow and started dragging Cindy across the forest towards the house.

"I can't believe you slipped out of the house—right under my nose. Your father would be turning in his grave if he knew that you were kissing some strange man. Anyone could have heard you out there, stupid, stupid girl. I'll lock you up in the attic and you can stay there forever!" her stepmother shouted.

The truth was that Cindy wasn't all that scared of her stepmother, but all of a sudden she felt sober, alerted that she was out in the darkness. Her thoughts began to race and she couldn't put together a coherent response, suddenly paralysed by fear.

In the past when her father was still alive, she was always happy and cheerful. She lived in a big home with a stunning garden and a few outbuildings. She didn't remember her mother much, since she died when Cindy was young. Her father was a very good man, and he looked after her well.

Several years later, when Cindy turned thirteen her father remarried. Ida was a divorcee with two daughters. Apparently she met her father at the market in another kingdom when Ted was trying to sell her an expensive rug.

Ida had been after Ted's money from the beginning and only married him because he was wealthy. She had prearranged the perfect plan of seduction and after weeks of seeing him, he finally proposed. Cindy knew the truth; once she overheard

Teresa and Susan talking about it and laughing about how her father had been so clueless. As Cindy grew older, her father felt guilty leaving her alone when he travelled, and he wanted her to have company—that's why he married Ida.

One day after a month of absence, a telegram arrived. Ida told Cindy that her father had a heart attack and died on the road. It was one of the worst days of her life and she was truly devastated.

"You are ruining your reputation, Cindy. No one will ever want you once the rumours spread that you're making out with strangers in the bushes," Ida was saying when they were just outside the house, but Cindy wasn't listening to her anymore. She was still humiliated. Eventually, she ran up to her room in the attic. She didn't even have a chance to explain herself to Charles and now she had no idea when she would see him again.

Several minutes later, Ida followed her to her room, which didn't happen very often.

"I know what I'm doing. Charles thinks I'm beautiful, and you can't keep telling me what to do. I'm an adult now," she replied hastily, trying to tidy up her closet to take her mind off what happened in the forest. She had no idea what had gotten into her today, but she'd never talked back to her stepmother before.

Ida looked surprised and Cindy thought that maybe it was about time she stood up for herself. She'd let this woman treat her like garbage for too many years.

"You...don't be stupid. Men will always want obedient wives and you're a spoiled brat who doesn't know how to behave. Your father asked me to take care of you, and I'm doing this for your own good," Ida said, brushed her forehead and then barged out the door, muttering something about responsibility and attitude.

Cindy laughed, shaking her head. She was afraid that the forest ranger would never speak to her again. She thought about running away or breaking out, but then what? She had no idea where to go and Ida was her guardian until she was officially married.

She decided to worry about it tomorrow. She was tired after the night's events and utter humiliation. She changed into her nighty, then slipped under the thin covers. The bed was old and not very comfortable, but Cindy wanted to stay positive, thinking of better days to come.

She closed her eyes and started to imagine her first real date with Charles and him making love to her. Cindy wasn't stupid, and she knew that Charles was the one for her. She was ready to sleep with him, because she knew that it felt right. He would never let her down. Her stepmother was wrong. Cindy wasn't a slut. She would only gift her virtue to someone she truly loved.

All of her dreams were suddenly interrupted by the sound of horses outside. Cindy threw back the covers and ran to the window to see who was paying her stepmother a visit so late at night. Her heart skipped a beat when she saw a royal carriage with snow white horses. Shortly after, the coachman stepped out and greeted her stepmother in front of the house. He was dressed in a white uniform and Cindy instantly remembered that some women at the market were saying that Prince Eric's father, King Caspian, was planning to organise a ball for his son. Apparently, he was fed up that the prince wasn't even considering settling down, and he wanted him to find a wife.

The coachman smiled politely towards her stepmother and handed her something that looked like an invitation. That letter could only mean one thing—King Caspian had finally made up his mind and organised a ball. Cindy's eyes sparkled with excitement as she watched how the coachman handed her mother four envelopes. Yes, she couldn't have been wrong, she saw four letters, which meant that one was for her.

There was no way that her stepmother would make a decision about Cindy attending the ball or not. And if she tried, Cindy would find a way to sneak out or run. Either way her spirits were soaring. She was going to the ball no matter what, because this was her only chance to meet with the forest ranger —the man she knew she would eventually love.

Chapter Two

"I haven't been this excited since the butcher from the village told me he would go down on me," Susan said, giggling like she was just about to have a fit.

Cindy was behind the house, collecting feed for the chickens when she overheard Susan talking yet again about her sexual adventures with various men that she used to meet in town. Both of Cindy's stepsisters had no idea that she could hear them talking from around the corner. It was a long day and Cindy had hidden in the old part of the house, hoping to rest for a bit while she finished feeding the chickens, but it seemed like Susan and Teresa had a similar idea.

Her stepmother had given her a list of menial chores that she needed to complete by dawn, and threatened to kick her out of the house if she didn't finish on time. Cindy was used to her stepmother's bullying tactics, but things had gotten a bit worse since she'd snuck out to the tavern a few days ago.

Cindy shook her head, not quite believing what she was hearing. She knew her stepsisters weren't afraid of their mother, and she didn't really care. Cindy wasn't the kind of person who judged people, especially her stepsisters. They also didn't seem to care what people thought about them. She knew her stepsisters slept around with random men while her stepmother thought they were perfectly well-mannered ladies who would preserve their virtue until marriage—if she only knew half of what they did, she'd be scandalised.

"I know, attending a royal ball is so exciting. I bet we'll see many fit guys over there," Teresa squeaked.

"Pfff, forget about the other guys. Prince Eric is the hottest of them all. I need to find a way to talk to him, and once we get past that, then I can show him my idea of a good time in his bedroom," Susan said, already planning her usual seduction game.

Cindy rolled her eyes. Did Susan really think the prince would just leave with her during the ball? There would be a hundred-plus ladies standing by for introduction and he would be obligated to make time for everyone.

Ida didn't tell Cindy that she had gotten an invitation for the ball, and Cindy was worried. She was certain that her stepmother wouldn't allow her to attend, claiming that she was never invited.

She was planning to talk to her stepmother about it as soon as possible. Her stepsisters were very unpleasant to her today, calling her a whore and a slut. They probably heard what had happened with the forest ranger and they were simply jealous. Cindy didn't understand why Susan and Teresa treated her so badly. She had never done anything bad to them in any way and she always covered for them when they snuck out.

Deep down, she felt bad that she ran away to see the forest ranger last night, but she knew that she wasn't going to meet anyone while being locked up in the house forever.

It was the king who organised the ball for his son. Apparently, the young prince was ruining the king's reputation and the ball was Caspian's last chance to put him back on the right path. King Caspian wanted him to find a suitable wife and finally settle down.

"I'm going to be there too, you know, so don't jump the hoop yet. I give much better head than you," Teresa said confidently and her sister snorted automatically as if to disagree. "Besides, only yesterday I slept with the squire who's been flirting with me for so long. He was all right, but he had a bit of a trouble getting it up, you know. And Mommy is so uptight these days. She really needs to find herself a new husband. She needs to chill out a bit."

"Don't be silly. Mum won't get married again. Ted was the last one, and he was so naive. Shame that he had to have a daughter. Cindy is such a slut. The other night Mum caught her with the forest ranger in the bushes. Can you believe it?"

Cindy angrily clenched her fists, breathing hard. Of course, her stepsisters knew about her date with Charles. Ida must have told them everything to teach Cindy a lesson.

She filled up a bucket of water and turned around, going back to her chickens. Susan and Teresa could sleep with whomever they wanted, but they needed to stop making her life difficult. One day she had been polishing the floor in the kitchen, and once she was done Teresa and Susan purposely walked inside with their muddy shoes to get a drink. Then her stepmother noticed her standing around and looking miserable, so she started shouting at her while her stepsisters laughed. Cindy remembered many similar incidents. Her stepsisters just adored making her life as difficult as it could be.

"Soon, I'm going to fall in love with a wonderful man who will love me back, and get married. My stepmother won't crush my hopes and dreams," Cindy said to herself, and then smiled thinking about Charles, hoping he would wait for her at the ball.

***

A week had passed since Cindy was dragged away from the bushes by her stepmother and she still hadn't heard from Charles. She was expecting him to visit her or at least send her a letter to let her know that he was thinking about her. He was so eager the other night to meet with Ida and talk to her about Cindy, so Cindy was positive that he liked her. She wanted to believe that he would continue to pursue her, but now she was confused about his silence.

On top of everything, her stepmother was piling more and more responsibilities on her with each passing day. She barely had time to sleep. Sometimes Cindy couldn't even catch her breath, she was so busy cleaning and cooking.

Susan and Teresa had been telling her that Ida wasn't going to let her go to the ball, but she kept ignoring them. She saw the invitation, but she had yet to hold it in her hands and was afraid that her stepmother had torn it to pieces out of spite.

Cindy hadn't talked to her stepmother about the ball, but she knew she needed to do it eventually—she couldn't avoid it forever. Time was running out and she still didn't have a dress ready. A few days before the ball, late at night when she could barely keep her eyes open, she tried to create something out of some her old dresses. Piece by piece, she tried to sew an elaborate gown from what she had, but the more she stared at the dress the more she thought it was a waste of time. The dress was falling apart and the material was worn out. She hated the bland colour, but the white dress that she had stolen a few days ago was now ruined by Cindy's constant alterations. She just couldn't attend the ball looking like a maid or a servant.

On Thursday she was carrying two buckets of water to the kitchen, considering going through her stepsisters' wardrobe.

Her thoughts were interrupted by a noise from outside. She heard someone arriving, so she went out to the porch, wondering if her stepmother was expecting anyone. Moments later, the horses stopped abruptly, and Cindy saw an old school carriage that had seen better days.

She saw a man who was struggling to squeeze through the door of the carriage. His coachman was staring at the man inside, looking pretty amused, and playing with a whip in his hand. The guest had very short legs, and a huge stomach. Eventually he slammed on the ground, ending up in a pile of mud and cursing loudly. Cindy couldn't help herself, and laughed a little. The man swore a few more times, finally pulling himself back to his feet.

The guest looked like the sort of person that didn't have much money, but Cindy knew he wasn't a peasant either. She didn't like judging people by the way they looked, but she did notice that he was quite clumsy and carrying a few extra pounds. He picked a large black hat up off the ground and put it back on his head.

"Hello, welcome to our home. How can I help you?" Teresa asked, suddenly appearing by Cindy.

She wore a very short skirt that her mother wouldn't approve of, and was smiling at the stranger, fluttering her eyelashes.

Teresa had long ginger hair and a large jaw. Today Cindy noticed that she put an awful lot of makeup on to cover all of her freckles. Teresa must have realised that she wasn't one of the most beautiful girls, but she wasn't lacking anything in the chest area. Her boobs were large and she always wore revealing tops that showcased her cleavage.

The man jumped and nearly fell into the mud again, but somehow he managed to keep his balance this time around. Teresa giggled to herself, lifted her boobs with both hands and walked confidently towards the stranger. Cindy noticed that her stepsister didn't really care if the man that she was just about to flirt with was good looking or not. She would try to seduce him either way. Nothing or no one had ever stopped her from having fun.

The large stranger's eyes immediately went to her boobs and he smiled like a kid on Christmas morning. Cindy noticed that he was missing one front tooth and she shuddered with repulsion.

"Yes, I need to see Miss Ida, the milkman in town informed me that she lives here," he replied, trying to make himself look decent, but failing. His clothes were filthy, covered in mud.

"Teresa, don't just stand out there and look pretty. Invite our guest into the living room!" Cindy's stepmother shouted from the porch, startling her.

"Please, please come in. My mother will be right with you," Teresa quickly said, smiling.

Cindy shook her head and carried on with her work. Then she went to the kitchen. She still needed to cook dinner for everyone. She had no idea who the newcomer was and didn't really care.

Her head was filled with thoughts about the ball, and she couldn't concentrate on anything else. The ball was only a few days away and she needed to find a beautiful dress to impress Charles. Ida couldn't just forbid her to attend; maybe in the past she'd let her dominate her, but not this time—Cindy was going to ball with or without her stepmother's permission.

Sometime later when she was peeling the potatoes and singing to herself in the kitchen, her other stepsister Susan barged in looking flustered.

"Mother is asking for you. She told me to tell you to make yourself look presentable and not to keep her waiting for too long," Susan stated, then tossed her black hair behind her and vanished before Cindy could ask her what Ida wanted from her.

Since that incident in the forest her stepmother barely exchanged more than a few words with Cindy. Ida couldn't keep her in the attic forever. She didn't have any help and since her father passed away she'd fired all of the servants. Cindy was the only one who was doing the daily chores around the house.

She quickly washed her hands and headed to the living room, smoothing her silver blond hair. On a good day, Cindy thought that she was pretty. She had a slim figure that she inherited from her mother, pale complexion and wide, azure blue eyes. Her friend Red, in the past, had told her that she needed to be more confident if she wanted to catch a husband.

Pamela believed that women shouldn't be dominated by men in any way and Cindy liked the idea. At the same time, she wasn't sure if she could be like Red. She wasn't that self-assured.

Her purple dress was filled with stains, but she didn't have time to change. Her stepmother was already waiting for her. Cindy used to have good clothes, amazing dresses that her father used to bring her from all of his travels. However, once her stepmother started treating her like a maid, Teresa and Susan took her dresses away, saying that she wouldn't need them anymore.

Five minutes later, she entered the living room. Her stepmother was sitting on the sofa with a cup of tea in her hand. The male guest was opposite her, looking bored. Cindy thought that he was even more unattractive from her angle and wondered what kind of business her stepmother needed from him. The man had a wide head, was mostly bald, and looked to be around Cindy's age or maybe just a bit older.

"You called me, stepmother," Cindy said.

Ida narrowed her eyes at her and sipped the tea through her pursed lips. Her brown hair was tied up in a tight bun, and she wore a long black dress. In any other circumstances, Cindy would have to say that her stepmother was an attractive woman, but the sour expression on her face made her unappealing.

"Sit down, Cindy, there is something that I have to discuss with you," she ordered.

Cindy obeyed her stepmother and sat down opposite her, placing her palms on her knees. The man stared at her with a stupid grin on his face, like he just won a prize.

"So, is this the girl? Very pretty, and young. She should adapt well to my farm. Although, she doesn't seems very strong, my lady. It's hard work, you know," the man said and her stepmother sighed.

Cindy had no idea what he was talking about and for some reason she wasn't eager to find out.

"Cindy, this is Mr. Londis and he's looking to find a suitable wife for himself," her stepmother stated. "We met in town and I suggested that you two should meet to discuss the further details of marriage. I believe that you will be perfectly suited to him."

For a split second Cindy thought that she must have misheard her stepmother. She couldn't have suggested what she thought.

A wife?

The man wanted a wife and Ida thought about Cindy.

She must be dreaming. Cindy couldn't marry a man like that. First of all, she didn't even love him and second of all, she didn't even know him. It wasn't even about his looks, but everything else.

She heard a giggle coming from the door behind her and noticed her stepmother exhale sharply. Cindy realised that her stepsisters were listening to what was going on in the living room. All of a sudden she felt nauseous and wanted to run back to her room.

"But, stepmother, there must be some mistake. I didn't ask you to find me a husband," she said. You could cut the tension in the air with a knife. Her stepmother shot her an annoyed glare and stretched her lips further.

"This isn't up for discussion, Cindy. A girl your age should be settling down and Mr. Londis is available. He has a certain reputation in the neighbouring town. If you're going to picky about it, you'll never find a husband for yourself." Ida said, sounding furious that Cindy was actually questioning her.

"Yes…uhm…there's so much that needs doing on the farm I inherited from my father. And I've been looking for the right woman for so long. Maybe if your stepmother will allow it, I could take you away with me, show you around. My home is very nice, but requires a woman's touch, a good homemaker," Mr. Londis said, smiling and revealing some of his missing teeth. Cindy cringed.

This was a horrible mistake, an error on Ida's part. She couldn't possibly marry someone like Londis. What was her stepmother thinking?

That man was unattractive and not suited to her at all.

"Of course you can take her away with you. Cindy would love to see everything for herself, wouldn't you, Cindy? I think this is a tremendous idea," Ida said pointedly, raising her perfectly sculpted eyebrows, and Cindy thought she was going to throw up as the reality of the situation began looming over her.

"Stepmother, I don't think I'm ready for such a huge step. May I speak to you privately?" Cindy asked, but her head was spinning and her thoughts were racing a mile a minute. She couldn't possibly leave with this man, this stranger.

"Nonsense, of course you're ready," her stepmother snapped and then touched her head. "Oh, I suddenly don't feel very well. Cindy, can you go and fetch me a glass of water. I think it's my migraine flaring up again."

Cindy wasn't listening, but part of her stepmother's request reached her ears. She stood up and left the living room as fast as she could. Her world was crashing down all around her, and she was losing control.

She nearly tripped over something, but managed to keep her balance. Then she heard giggling and noticed that Teresa's foot was sticking out. She purposely tried to trip Cindy.

"It looks like Mommy is going to sell your arse to that fatty over there. I bet you can't wait to suck him off, right?" Susan giggled and Cindy wanted to slap her. She wasn't a violent person in general, but at that moment she felt a potent anger rising deep inside her stomach.

"There is no way I'm going to agree to marry that man. Your mother is crazy and I'm not an idiot. There's a man out there who's just right for me and it's not him," Cindy shouted, knowing her stepmother most likely had heard her, but she didn't care anymore. She had had enough of being treated like she couldn't make a decision for herself.

"Too bad that she already made a deal with him. Besides, the forest ranger is way out of your league, so you better start looking for a nice wedding dress. Your future's already decided."

Cindy clenched her fists, trying to breathe at the same time, and left the room before she did something she'd regret later. She wasn't going to do what her stepmother wanted, even if she had to run away.

Chapter Three

Over the next two days, Cindy couldn't stop thinking about Mr. Londis and the fact that her stepmother was rushing her into the marriage. She knew Ida and she realised that she wouldn't simply let Cindy choose the man she wanted to marry. She needed to act fast, figure out a way to get out of this absurd arrangement.

Her stepmother didn't mention Mr. Londis again, but Cindy wasn't stupid. She was even considering running away to another kingdom or asking for help from someone else. Realistically, she knew that she didn't have any money. Her father had left her the house, but Ida was still in charge of the whole estate.

Teresa and Susan kept teasing her about Londis, and she kept telling herself that she still had options. Charles was single, and there were other men in the village that were much more suited to her than Londis. She was going to get married either way, but only to a man she truly loved and cared for. Her stepmother knew that Cindy wouldn't like Londis at all. She wanted to get rid of her anyway, and marrying her off was the perfect opportunity.

Things started getting a bit complicated when the next day Ida brought in a new cook and told Cindy to show her everything in the kitchen. It looked like Ida wasn't wasting any time and Cindy really needed to talk to her about attending the ball. However, every time she tried, someone always interrupted her. And her stepsisters were sabotaging all of her cleaning duties, creating a mess and leaving a pile of dirty clothes for her to wash. She knew that Susan and Teresa were testing her limits, and they wanted her to snap, but she wasn't planning to give them the satisfaction.

The day of the ball was approaching quicker than she anticipated and day after day Cindy had been coming back to her room exhausted. Ida was giving her more cleaning duties and also training the new cook/maid was extremely draining. She had no time for anything else. After all her daily chores were done, Cindy was too tired to even think about sewing a new dress for the ball. On top of that, she saw the forest ranger with Pamela at the market on Friday, and it crushed her even more. She didn't understand what had happened. The two of them broke up, and Charles couldn't have already forgotten about her.

Cindy was furious with herself and heartbroken, but she told herself that maybe he and Red were only friends. And after what happened between them, she was certain that he would choose to take her to the ball. They hadn't talked about it, but Cindy knew once she showed up at his house looking beautiful, he wouldn't say no to her.

The night before the ball, she found a storage box that hadn't been used since her father passed away. She finally had something to work with. Some of the materials were in good shape, and she knew she could create something spectacular if she had a bit more time. She ran back to the attic once all of her work was complete and started thinking about the dress she wanted to create. After a few minutes she felt exhausted and knelt down to rest for a bit. Every muscle in her body was aching badly. She had lifted, carried, cleaned and mopped for hours while her stepmother had just been adding things that needed to be done.

Cindy closed her eyes and before she knew it, she was drifting off to sleep, not even realising it was already dark outside.

The next day, bright beams of sunlight woke her up. She jumped to her feet, having no idea why she was still in her clothes, and not in her nightgown.

"No, no, I couldn't have fallen asleep," she whispered to herself, seeing that the old dresses from the storage were on the floor. She realised that last night she was so exhausted, she must have fallen asleep, kneeling down. She was ready to cry, knowing that her plan had fallen to pieces. The ball was starting in several hours and she didn't even have a dress.

When she glanced at the clock she saw that it was nearly eleven a.m. She was surprised that no one had barged into her room, telling her that she was already late with her duties. Cindy went downstairs and realised that her stepmother and stepsisters must have left early to pick up their dresses from the shop in town. Cindy had a lot of work today, but this was the perfect opportunity to create her dress for the ball. She didn't hesitate this time, and picked out whatever she could from her stepsisters' rooms. Teresa and Susan had lots of dirty dresses scattered around the floor and Cindy assumed that they wouldn't miss some old forgotten clothes, so she took what she needed.

She found her sewing kit in the cupboard that used to belong to her mother and started making a dress for her first ball. In the past, she used to make dresses for her dolls; her father had brought someone from town that showed her how to use the sewing machine.

Cindy didn't care that the house wasn't cleaned and that the cook was waiting for her in the kitchen. Her dream was finally coming together and she wasn't going to waste any time this morning. Finding a suitable husband, someone other than Londis, was tops on the list of her priorities.

Several hours later, her dress was ready and Cindy was extremely proud of herself. She kept staring at the silver material, imagining dancing with a real prince. Eventually, her stepmother and stepsisters came back, but they didn't even pay attention to her. Ida looked stressed about last minute errands that she needed to run, while Susan and Teresa were running around, panicking that they were going to get to the castle too late. None of them had men who would accompany them to the ball. Cindy knew that they were hoping the prince would notice them standing alone in the crowd of other women.

She started cleaning to keep her mind off the fact that she still had to talk to Ida to get her permission. The sun was slowly setting and her stomach was suddenly in knots. She didn't know how she was going to get to the ball in the first place.

Cindy looked anxiously at the window, thinking she might be to be too afraid to leave the house on her own.

"Cindy, come here right away. I need you to curl my hair," Teresa called from the other room. Cindy was happy to help her. She had her dream dress ready to go, and she knew that she could sneak away from the house after Ida and the girls left. Her plan was coming together nicely.

"Oh, I really hope that the prince won't be a spoiled brat and he'll actually dance with us. There will be other ladies there, but after all, we do come from such a good family. We're bound to hit it off," Teresa was saying to Cindy, wearing a very bright pink dress while putting powder on her cheeks. Cindy was curling her hair, nodding, but her mind was elsewhere.

"He might choose me for sure," Susan stated, rolling her eyes at her sister's words while brushing her hair.

They started to argue about who was better looking. Soon, just as Cindy predicted, their argument turned into a catfight. The girls were shouting at each other while Cindy wondered if she had shoes that would look good with her dress.

"Ladies, we are leaving in five minutes," Ida said, walking into the room all of a sudden. Her eyes automatically moved down to Cindy who was just about to sneak upstairs to change too. If everything went according to plan, she would get to the forest ranger's home. She wasn't sure if he was back together with Red or not, but she was still convinced that he would take her to the ball. Cindy still shivered thinking about the way Charles had kissed and touched her. Their connection and chemistry was real. "Cindy there's a little present waiting for you upstairs in your room. You've been working really hard over the past few days and I wanted to reward you. I have your invitation to the ball, and I think you should come with us."

Cindy looked at her stepmother like she'd grown a pair of horns. She couldn't believe Ida would notice her hard work. Maybe she wasn't that bad after all and wanted her to have a good time at the ball. She couldn't believe that her stepmother had just thanked her. That had never happened before.

"Thank you, stepmother," Cindy mumbled, feeling really happy that everything turned out so well. She didn't want to go against her stepmother wishes and run away to the ball without her permission. Besides, she was too afraid of the dark to go on her own.

She ran back upstairs to change into her new dress, but when she got there she saw her dress was completely torn apart. No. This is just a bad dream. Blood rushed to her ears. Tears slipped down her cheek as she picked up the pieces that she had carefully sewn for hours. Everything was ruined. She couldn't save it. The door to her attic room was unlocked most of the day, so anyone could have walked in there.

"Now you understand the consequences of crossing me, you stupid girl. The prince would have never looked at you anyway, because you are too poor and uninteresting," her stepmother said, smiling viciously. "You stole all the materials from my daughters and that simply isn't acceptable. I won't tolerate thievery. Your wedding to Mr. Londis is going to happen whether you like it or not."

Ida was dressed in a beautiful shiny blue dress. Teresa and Susan were standing behind her laughing at Cindy as the tears poured down her face.

"Yeah, you were never invited to the ball, so I have no idea what you were thinking. You're just a maid," Teresa added, tossing her curly red hair behind her, and they all walked away giggling.

Ida slammed her door shut and Cindy threw herself on the bed, sobbing even harder. She couldn't believe that her stepmother could be so cruel—ruining her dress to make sure Cindy couldn't go to the ball. What had she ever done to deserve such cruelty?

Cindy wasn't ready to marry a man she didn't love, just because her stepmother wanted to get rid of her. And she knew Londis would have her working twice as hard and just as long as she did there.

Cindy cried and cried until she had no more tears left. Eventually she got up and went to the window. She saw a bright, radiant light emanating from the castle in the distance and imagined herself dancing at the ball with Charles.

She wiped her nose and tried to calm down, thinking rationally about everything that had happened. Her thoughts started racing away and the tiny voice in her head told her that she couldn't give up just yet. Cindy wasn't ready to sit in her room and sulk all night while her stepsisters were dancing and having a good time. She had been dreaming about this kind of opportunity for far too long.

Minutes later, she got up, put the torn dress back into the wardrobe, and washed her face. After everything that she'd been through she wasn't going to let Ida win or get away with selling her like she was a piece of chattel.

Cindy threw her coat on and went downstairs, feeling a little better. She located her invitation to the ball, hidden in her stepmother's wardrobe. She pressed it to her heart and felt a bit braver. Then she went to the door and took a few deep breaths staring out into the darkness. Her heart started pounding in her chest. She remembered the moment when the coachman brought news about her father's death. It was the middle of the night and she had just woken up from a real nightmare. When her stepmother broke the news, she was paralysed. Cindy couldn't believe that her father wasn't coming back. Since that night every time she tried to leave the house, her anxiety gripped her tightly. She felt suffocated and couldn't breathe.

Tonight her pulse spiked as soon as she took a step outside the house and her breathing became laboured. For several moments, she tried to pull herself together, but it wasn't easy. After about half an hour of mental anguish, she managed to get to the gate. She felt her heart jackhammering in her chest as old fears wrenched her stomach. The world around her began spinning like a merry-go-round, but she told herself that she could do this—she had to. If she wanted to go to the ball she had to keep going.

"Charles is waiting for you in his house," she told herself. "Knowing Red, she went to the ball with someone else. It's only a ten-minute walk from here." But fear rose in the pit of her stomach, paralysing her further. The forest was dangerous, filled with wild animals, but Cindy had to keep walking. No one ever told her that this was going to be easy—she had to face her fears.

Small beads of sweat were dripping down her face. She had no idea how long she'd been walking, but she was taking one step at the time. When she looked up she saw dark clouds appearing in the sky and she felt that it might rain soon. It was getting colder, the temperature dropping down at an alarming rate. Charles's home wasn't too much further and she already knew what she was going to tell him.

Then she heard something in the bushes and fear rooted her to the spot. Seconds started to drag by and Cindy couldn't move. A trickle of fear moved through her veins.

She shut her eyes and waited for the beast or a monster to attack. Just another reason why she hated going out in the night.

Five or ten minutes later she realised that she was still breathing—there was no monster. Her vision went slightly blurry, so she thought about happy times, mainly when her father was still alive, and managed to take a few more steps.

About half an hour later, she found herself outside the forest ranger's home. There was a light shining in the windows and Cindy thought that she had been saved at last. She wanted to cry, knowing she had made huge progress tonight overcoming her fear of the dark, walking in the forest alone.

She was just about to leave her hiding place and knock on his door when she saw Charles. And he wasn't alone. Red Riding Hood was with him and she looked absolutely beautiful, wearing a purple shiny dress with tiny diamonds scattered around the full length of the skirt. Charles was staring at her like he was in love, and something inside Cindy's chest cracked. Her heart burst and she felt a little dizzy. She couldn't believe that Charles hooked up with Pamela again. It wasn't fair, especially not after what he had been telling her. They had met countless times and she was ready to give him his virtue.

Cindy might have an invitation, but she knew she looked like a maid, not a future princess. There was no way she could show up at the ball wearing her old dress. Charles wore a sharp military-style jacket and brown leather pants, and he looked really handsome.

Cindy watched how Charles smiled at Red Riding Hood, helping her to their carriage. They laughed at one another and held on to each other intimately. Moments later, the horses pulled the carriage away, leaving Cindy completely alone in the darkness.

She burst into tears and threw her invitation to the ball on the ground, knowing that she had to get back home. She had no idea what she was thinking. She couldn't walk into the castle looking like a servant. Hot tears were streaming down her face and bitter disappointment filled her heart. Cindy had never been so miserable in her entire life. It looked like her dream was never going to be fulfilled. Not after Charles shattered her heart to a billion different pieces.

Chapter Four

Cindy was really worried. She was lost in the deep, dark forest, unable to find her way back to the house. Meanwhile, her stepmother and stepsisters were on their way to the ball. Cindy was trying to find a silver lining in the whole situation. She thought that being lost in the dark wasn't the worst thing that ever happened to her. No, that would come in a few weeks when she would be marrying a man she didn't love and she would be stuck with him for the rest of her life. Ida was selling her off like a cheap product she owned, and she hated it. Cindy was owned by no one—least of all her stepmother.

After taking a few deep breaths, she forced herself to continue walking. A chill in the air ruffled her hair and she swallowed hard, trying to overcome the absurd fear of darkness surrounding her. Several steps later, she tripped over something. Cindy went down, rolled on the ground, and ended up in spiky bushes. For a split second, her head was spinning, then she was certain she heard someone nearby.

"Auuu, my fucking head. I'm going to kill Eliza for that tequila."

In any other circumstance she would have laughed, but she was still pretty freaked out. She managed to get up off the ground and slowly find her way out of the bushes. It was pitch black, but a few meters away from her, she saw a woman on the ground, who was trying to lift herself up but seemed to struggle a bit.

"Who are you?" Cindy asked, a little baffled but willing to keep an open mind. The woman finally sat up and pushed a mass of her curly red hair out of her eyes. Cindy thought that she was dressed a bit too provocatively, considering it was freezing cold outside. She was wearing a very low cut, corset-type dress, her boobs were practically popping out, and she had very intense makeup on.

The woman noticed her after a long moment. She rubbed her eyes and then burped loudly.

"Where the hell am I?" she asked Cindy, then lifted a bottle of tequila and took a generous gulp. She pressed her eyes together, and Cindy realised that the alcohol most likely burned her throat. She shuddered with revulsion, remembering her father drinking it too, but only in small amounts.

"Wow, this shit is strong," the woman muttered to herself, still ignoring Cindy.

"Don't mind me, I'm just going to be on my way. No one cares if a wild animal eats me alive out here," Cindy said as she got up and tried to take another step, but found that she couldn't.

More tears streamed down her cheeks, and she felt frustrated with herself and her inability to even find the way home.

"Hey, where are you going and why the hell are you sobbing like a little child?" the woman asked Cindy, finally realising that she wasn't alone. "Help me up, will you? My dress is so heavy."

Cindy was planning to ignore her, but she thought better of it. She took a deep breath, walked back to the stranger, and helped her to stand back up.

"Thank you, pretty girl. My name is Martha," the woman said, giving her a bright smile as she lifted her boobs up. Cindy liked Martha's long dress and the silly gloves that she wore. What she didn't like was the odour of alcohol that wafted from her—it was toxic. "What has you so upset that you're in the forest alone, sobbing like that?"

"The darkness always scares me to the point of unbridled fear, but I forced myself to go out tonight. I walked all the way to the forest ranger's home, hoping that he would take me to the ball at the castle," Cindy explained, telling herself to get it together. She wasn't alone anymore, so there was no point freaking out.

"The ball...fuck, my head is killing me. I shouldn't have trusted that stupid locksmith. I knew he would run away without paying me first. What a moron," Martha said, trying to smooth her red hair. "The ball? What ball are you talking about?"

Cindy frowned, wondering where the hell Martha had been in the past two weeks. Everyone in the Farrington Kingdom was aware that King Caspian was throwing a ball for his son. People at the market and on the street hadn't talked about anything else. Posters were everywhere, and Cindy wondered if maybe Martha had travelled from another kingdom tonight.

"King Caspian organised a ball in order to find a suitable wife for his son, Eric. I had an inv..."

Cindy didn't finish what she meant to say. She went down on her knees to find the invitation that she threw away earlier. Luckily, it was by the tree, but it was so dark when she handed it to Martha, she could barely read what was written on it.

"Oh yeah, that stupid thing. And that's why you're crying, because some loser took another girl to the ball?" Martha asked, and took another sip of her drink, then closed her eyes really hard and burped again. Cindy nodded her head. She felt a bit silly when Martha put it that way.

"I live with my stepmother and stepsisters. My father was a very rich..."

She didn't really want to tell Martha what had been going on with her lately, but once she started talking the words started pouring out of her. She talked about her father's passing, then about her stepmother, her dreams, and ended her story when she tripped over Martha's foot. Cindy had no idea if Martha was even interested in her life, but she kept talking, feeling better about herself by the minute. At least she didn't have to bury all those feelings inside any longer. It felt good to finally tell someone.

Once she was done, she realised that she wasn't scared or even sad anymore. For some reason she was ready to head home on her own.

"What's your name?" Martha asked after a moment of silence.

"Cindy."

"Well, Cindy, I tell you what, you sound like a nice and reasonable young woman. That stepmother of yours is an arsehole and those stepsisters…well, they are just whores. Plain and simple. I worked in the local brothel, so I'm not exactly a shining example of someone who knows what she's talking about, but come with me. My mother was real fairy and I do have magic running through my veins. Maybe we can figure something out together. But first things first, I need to find a cure for this awful hangover," Martha explained and drank a bit more of what Cindy guessed was most likely tequila.

Cindy had no idea what to think or do, but she knew for sure that she didn't want to just give up and return to her house. It was probably late and the ball had already started, but she could still go. She realised Martha was a hooker, but Cindy didn't care—she wanted to meet the prince.

"Go where? I don't understand any of it, besides I have nothing to wear. Look at me," she said, ready to burst into tears again. Martha laughed, and her huge boobs bounced up and down. Cindy didn't think it was funny at all. Her misery was her own doing.

"Come on, I'll sort you out; my magic is whispering that I should help you," Martha stated, grabbed Cindy by her elbow, and started dragging her across the forest, far away from the forest ranger's home. Cindy was apprehensive, knowing that she needed transportation to the ball as well. The disappointment of seeing Charles with Red was still drilling holes in her gut, but Cindy couldn't just give up like that.

Cindy thought that her father would turn in his grave if he saw her like this, lost and miserable. "I can't believe that your stepmother would want to marry you off to some toothless, fat loser. She's a right bitch, but I have no idea why you keep letting her treat you like a slave. You should've stood up to her a long time ago."

Cindy didn't answer, but she knew that Martha was right. Ida was living in her house, eating her food, and spending her father's money. She knew that her father put some sort of clause in the will that allowed Ida to manage the estate, but Cindy had never actually been allowed to see the paperwork. She was thirteen when her father passed away and trusted her stepmother. Ida used the time when Cindy was lost in her grief to take full control of everything.

They kept going through the forest and now and again Martha would take sips from her bottle, telling Cindy to hurry up.

When they found their way back to the road, Cindy noticed that her heart wasn't pounding in her chest anymore. She was much calmer now, and able to walk just fine. Maybe it was because she was with Martha, she had no idea, but at that point she was glad her fears had dissipated. As they walked, Cindy found out that Martha was one of seven children to a peasant couple who lived in another kingdom. Her family was poor and Martha decided to leave their farm as soon as she was old enough to work. Later on, Martha learned that the peasant couple weren't her real parents at all. She was a changeling, the child of a fairy that had been left in place of a human child. Apparently, she found out about her parentage years later when her magical abilities started to manifest and get her into a lot of trouble. Unfortunately, she never found her real parents. Cindy thought that it was a bizarre story, but she decided not to voice her opinion. She didn't really believe in magic, but her father had told her that there were many other creatures on earth besides humans. Martha wanted to help her and she didn't want to offend her in any way, so she just went with it.

"Well, I had to earn a living somehow. The brothel in town was the only place that didn't stink and paid more than any job that I could've ever done, so here I am." She ended her story with a smile.

Cindy nodded with understanding and wasn't ready to judge her. She had enough on her plate as it was to worry about the fact that people in town might see her walking around with a hooker.

"I always wanted to fall in love, find a prince, and I've been planning my wedding ever since I was a little girl," Cindy explained as they finally reached town. The roads were empty and Cindy realised that it was most likely very late.

Martha snorted with laughter and patted Cindy on her back.

"A prince? Seriously, love, you need to get back to the real world. No one ever gets a prince. Just focus on getting a hot guy who has money and the rest will come," she said, shaking her head "All right, we're here. The girls will be so excited to meet you. I bet they're bored as hell because all the men are at the ball, accompanying the women from town."

Cindy smiled and told herself not to get her hopes up, because Martha couldn't really help her do anything. It was too late for her to get to the ball, and she still didn't have anything to wear.

They stopped in front of a wonky red building and walked inside. There was a small bar downstairs and at least five ladies were behind it, looking bored. They were all dressed in provocative dresses, and one of them was wearing only her underwear, almost falling asleep on the table. The strong smell of perfume wafted through the air, mixed with alcohol. Cindy could hardly believe she was actually in a brothel.

"Ladies, Martha's back and I have a job for y'all. This is Cindy and she needs our help to look fabulous this evening, so all of you move your sexy arses and take her upstairs. Cindy's going to the ball and planning to seduce the prince, so we need to make sure that he won't be able to take his eyes off her," Martha shouted, whistling loudly, and Cindy felt a little embarrassed. She wasn't planning to actually dance with the prince tonight. She was hoping to attend the ball with Charles.

All the girls jumped off their seats and started dragging Cindy upstairs, each of them talking at the same time. A few of them told Cindy that she had a great figure and a lot of men would go crazy over her huge boobs. She was trying to listen to all of them at the same time, but instead she just nodded, feeling a bit overwhelmed.

Before she could even explain what she wanted, the girls started pulling out beautiful dresses and removing her clothes. Cindy found herself in a large open room filled with colourful furnishings, cushions made up of various colours, small puffy chairs, and a table filled with all sorts of bottles. She was trying to protest, but in a matter of minutes she was standing in the middle of the room in only her underwear, while Giselle, one of the long-legged blondes started asking her which one of the five dresses she liked the most.

"I mean, this one is going to highlight your beautiful eyes, but I think red is going to make you stand out in the crowd. I've seen all the ladies wearing silver and cream tonight... so boring. And your boobs will look amazing in it," she explained, giggling away. Cindy wasn't sure if she wanted to show off her cleavage, but she didn't want to be rude, so she kept trying on dresses over and over until she put on a stunning, long red dress that accentuated her curves. It was shiny, with tiny inlaid crystals shimmering like diamonds throughout the entire gown. It made her feel like a real princess.

"And now we need to add jewellery and shoes," Martha said, scanning Cindy up and down. "Stick with me, girl, and you'll be just fine. And tomorrow when you get your prince, tell your stepmother to get lost."

Cindy didn't have a chance to thank Martha, because the other girls had sat her in a chair and started sorting out her hair and putting makeup on her face. Her long hair hung in tangled waves, because she never really had the time to brush them. It took a while for the girls to get her hair just right.

After an hour or maybe two, she stood in front of the mirror not recognising herself at all. Her blond hair was curled and pinned up in a fabulous bun; she wore long silky gloves and a beautiful red dress that shimmered in the soft lighting as if it were embodied with a thousand crystals. Someone had given her matching six-inch high heels, and as soon as she tried to walk in them, she struggled a bit, but overall she couldn't stop staring at herself in the mirror—the heels she'd have to get used to.

"Oh my lord, I look beautiful. I can't believe it," she whispered and tears began streaming down her cheeks.

"No, silly … don't you dare cry on me. You'll ruin all your makeup and we'll have to start over. Now come on, let's get you to that fucking ball," Martha shouted and all of a sudden all the girls were pushing her out of the door, talking at the same time again. She was moving through colourful corridors and then downstairs finally realising that she was really going to the ball and for the first time in her life she didn't have to worry about her stepmother.

Chapter Five

The girls and Martha took her outside the building. Cinderella was grateful for everything that Martha had done for her, but she still had no idea how she was going to get to the ball.

"I do appreciate the dress and everything else, but the castle is quite far away. I can't walk all that way in these shoes," she said, sounding a little apprehensive. She wasn't used to people being kind to her, and felt a little uneasy that Martha had done so much to help her.

"Don't worry, love, everything is under control. I'm a changeling not a human, remember? My magic's very powerful. I don't use it very often, but tonight I really want to see you arrive at the ball in style." Martha then brought two fingers to her mouth and whistled really loudly.

Cindy and the other girls looked like they had no idea what Martha was planning. They were all glancing around at each other, confusion in their eyes. Several moments later, two beggars came running from around the corner. Cindy couldn't believe that three poor men actually responded to Martha's whistle. They were filthy, toothless and Cindy thought they must have been living on the streets for years.

"Oi, you three stand still and try not moving for a bit. Both of you will go to sleep with full bellies tonight and you may even find some gold in your pockets tomorrow morning," Martha said with a smile. The beggars looked at each other shrugging their shoulders, and when Martha threw a huge piece of bread to each, they wolfed it down straight away. The poor men were starving.

Before Cindy and the rest of the girls could figure out what was going to happen next, Martha began dancing around, releasing a stream of colourful magic from her fingers. Warmth spread down Cindy's body, and she instantly felt happier, less anxious. Martha must have been telling Cindy the truth all along, because in a matter of seconds, the two beggars changed into splendid white horses. Electricity danced along her skin, lifting the tiny hairs on her body.

There were gasps and snippets of conversation amongst the girls, and Cindy stood by them widening her eyes.

"Right, ladies, give those two some straw, and I'll sort the carriage," Martha said, rubbing her palms together as she disappeared somewhere around the corner. Cindy's heart pounded in her chest as she tried to make sense of everything that had happened tonight. When Martha came back, Cindy was stroking the horses, thinking of what else the crazy hooker could be planning. The third man turned into a handsome coachman who bowed toward her.

The girls ran to Martha helping her pull an old trolley filled with rubbish and pieces of old furniture. Cindy was just about to ask Martha what she wanted to do with the trolley when a bright yellow light blinded her. There was a loud bang and then a burning smell wafted around.

Cindy coughed a few times, clearing her lungs, and when she looked up, the trolley was gone and in its place was a stylish white carriage with the two white horses in the lead. The coachman sat in front, holding a whip in his hand. All the girls looked impressed, completely awestruck, walking around and admiring it. Cindy was gobsmacked, but stopped questioning anything at that point. She was going to the ball, and nothing else mattered.

"Go on, girl, jump in and try to have a good time. You have until midnight, and then all the magic will disappear. Oh, and don't screw anyone while drunk." Martha winked, looking proud of her accomplishments.

Seconds later, Cindy hugged her, trying not to cry at the same time. She squeezed all the girls too, thanking them and saying that she would never forget them or their kindness.

"Right, go, go…otherwise you'll miss your prince," Martha kept saying, pushing her towards the carriage. The girls wished her good luck, and she waved to them as the horses pulled the carriage forward.

She sat back and tried to relax, wondering if it was too late to get to the ball. The journey to the castle took a while, and Cindy had no idea how the horses/beggars knew the way. She began to think that magic was most likely guiding them and told herself to stop worrying.

Finally, the carriage stopped in front of the royal castle. Cindy sat inside for a few minutes, trying to take it all in. Then a very handsome guard opened the door, smiling at her. He was dressed in a smart white uniform, and when she stepped out, he bowed in front of her. Carriages were still arriving, and Cindy knew she wasn't as late as she thought she was. She heard the orchestra playing inside and gazed up at the enormous castle that looked magnificent in the moonlight.

Cindy's heart pounded nervously in her chest as she followed other ladies and gents into the castle. When she walked inside the ballroom, what she saw was absolutely breathtaking—better than she could've ever imagined. There were tables decorated in black and white table coverings with intricately etched silver and gold lining, and elegant candle centrepieces. An elaborate chandelier accenting the entire ballroom, giving it a soft, enchanting glow. She noticed several couples dancing, but there were quite a few single ladies spread throughout the vast room, some were dancing, while others were drinking and eating. As she looked around, she began to recognise a lot of people from town. She knew that somehow she needed to keep far away from her stepmother and stepsisters.

She had no idea if Ida would recognise her looking so beautiful, but it was better to be careful. Soon, she spotted a group of ladies on the other side of the room surrounding someone who was engrossed in deep conversation. Cindy's interest was piqued and she decided to head over there to see what all the fuss was about. She noticed a few men were starting at her with interest, and smiling as she walked by. For now, she tried to ignore them, heat rising in the pit of her stomach—the last thing she needed was to blush crimson—the same colour as her dress. That would've been embarrassing.

It looked like the crowd of ladies was surrounding Prince Eric. Cindy was quite tall, but she had to wait several minutes in order to get to the front. There, she saw a man around her height who wore a gold uniform with royal symbols. Cindy recognised Prince Eric from the posters around town and she had to admit that he was quite handsome. He had short brown hair, high cheekbones, and bright hazel eyes.

"I don't know, ladies, it's hard to decide. There are so many of you here," the prince said. Cindy was amazed by how many girls were trying to get his attention. Most of them were smiling, giggling and waving at him. Two very pretty blondes were standing on each side, running their hands over his arm. "I must say that my good looks could easily overshadow all of you here. I don't want to sound too vain, but I'm just too handsome, and my wife has to be beyond beautiful."

Cindy frowned, thinking that Eric sounded exactly just as he had said—vain. She looked around, seeing that a lot of girls sighed loudly. Some were elbowing each other, trying to get closer to him.

"Yes, he's right. There isn't anyone here better looking than him," a girl on Cindy's right admitted, staring at Prince Eric like she was about to faint.

"I wish he would pick me to dance with him," another sighed. Cindy knew that she had heard enough and it was then when she realised that Eric didn't even notice her standing in front. His arrogant attitude didn't appeal to Cindy at all and she wondered why she wanted to meet him in the first place.

"My lord, look around. All these beautiful ladies here expect you to pick at least one of them to dance with you. Remember what your father said. He wants you to find a wife by the end of the night."

A shorter man dressed in a blue uniform was talking to Eric, reminding him of his responsibilities. Suddenly, two women pushed their way through to the front and Cindy's heart leapt to her throat when she realised that it was her stepsisters.

"I'll dance on my own if I have to; there isn't anyone worthy of my attention in here, Duncan. Maybe later I'll pick up a woman who won't steal all my glory." Cindy overheard Eric responding to the man who seemed to be his advisor.

She needed to disappear fast, knowing Teresa and Susan would make a scene if they recognised her. She didn't want to listen to the prince any longer. She thought his arrogance was appalling.

She proceeded to walk towards the drink table, wondering if she'd made a mistake by coming to the ball tonight. After all, the only man she was ever interested in brought his ex-girlfriend, Red Riding Hood, as his date.

Cindy drank some champagne, aware that after what happened in the forest she didn't want to risk walking back to the house on her own. The champagne tasted heavenly and Cindy knew she needed to eat something so she wouldn't get too tipsy. She turned around and saw Charles from across the room. He was waving his hand at Red and it seemed they were fighting about something. Other people were staring at them, and Cindy's heart sank when she saw Charles shake his head and walk away, leaving Red alone, looking completely miserable. It looked like their reunion was only temporary.

Charles didn't choose Cindy, and after his treatment of Red, she wasn't planning on taking advantage of the fact that he was alone again. Maybe it was time for her to get over him, and start talking to other men. The forest ranger just lost his usual appeal —he didn't know how to treat women and definitely wasn't the man Cindy thought he was.

She decided to head to the other side of the room, but then saw her stepmother walking towards her and Cindy panicked. She turned around abruptly with the intention of running, but instead she walked straight into someone.

Someone with a defined, muscular chest. Cindy swallowed hard and raised her eyes, meeting the gaze of a man who had the most mesmerising dark eyes that she had ever seen. Her heart jumped in her chest and slow waves of electricity zoomed throughout her body right down to her core. She gasped, realising that the man was much older than her, but he was incredibly handsome, with longish black hair and a wide jaw. Dressed in a sharp black suit, he outshined any other man at the ball.

All of a sudden, Cindy experienced tingles of heat between her thighs that instantly made her wet. He was taller than her, and something gleamed in his eyes, maybe surprise, astonishment, or even admiration. She wasn't sure, but she knew that her cheeks were most likely red by that point.

"Oh sorry... I didn't see you, I was just—"

"It's perfectly all right, nothing to be sorry about. On the contrary, I'm so glad to have bumped into such a beautiful creature. I feel incredibly fortunate," the stranger responded and smiled brightly. Another shot of unexpected desire jolted through her core again. Cindy was surprised and overwhelmed with intense feelings she'd never in her life experienced—she only felt like that when Charles was kissing her. This was something more primal, a sexual need, an unexpected craving for the man standing before her.

She couldn't stop staring at the handsome stranger. All she could think about was that she wanted to be ravaged by him— to have his hands and mouth all over her body. No, what the hell was wrong with her?

Just a second ago, she was running away from her stepmother, still thinking about Charles and Red. And now, she couldn't stop staring at some strange man—a gorgeous man, but a stranger nonetheless. She had no idea what to do with herself. She needed to disappear, but her legs seemed to be chained to the floor—she couldn't move.

"Thank you. My name is Cindy," she blurted out, aware that the man most likely wasn't going to care, but his eyes flickered with even more lust than before. Unexpectedly, the stranger took her hand and lowered his head, kissing it ever so gently. A shudder of excitement shot through her again, and she gasped for breath. There was something really wrong happening to her. She had never felt so overwhelmed with desire before. Was he dousing her with some kind of strange magic?

"It's a pleasure to meet you, Cindy. Is it short for Cinderella?"

She nodded, shocked that the man's voice sounded so sexy. She could listen to him speak all day long.

"My name is Caspian and I'm the father of Prince Eric. Please allow me to show you around. If I had known such a stunning woman would decide to show up at the ball I would have welcomed you at the door myself."

Cindy blushed even more, parting her lips. She couldn't believe that the prince's father, the king, had actually taken an interest in her. She didn't care about Eric at all; she thought he was narcissistic and vain anyway. The king, on the other hand, was well mannered and making her feel things she'd never felt in her life. Her heart was beating frantically in her chest, which wasn't normal. She never thought in a million years that King Caspian would be so incredibly good looking. She always thought of him as a decrepit, balding old man—not that she'd seen him of course, but her mind had a silly way of imagining things.

She bowed before him, forgetting about her stepmother or the fact that she was ready to leave.

"It's a pleasure to meet you, Your Highness," she said.

"No, please call me Caspian. I hate all of the formalities," he said. "Tonight's orchestra is very good. Would you like to dance with me?"

She felt like she was in a fog, unable to take a full control of her body. The king was asking her to dance. She couldn't talk, so she nodded instead. Moments later, they joined other couples on the dance floor. The king brought one arm around her waist and her whole body seared with heat. The fire in her core wouldn't stop burning.

"Stunning...you are absolutely stunning, Cindy, and I can't believe that our paths haven't crossed before," he said to her, moving his dark gaze down to her lips. Other couples were dancing around them and at some point, Cindy noticed Prince Eric. He was moving around the dance floor, pretending he was holding someone by his side. Some people laughed at him, but other girls were staring at him, still mesmerised.

"Thank you, I wasn't sure if I was going to make it," she said, as naughty images flashed in front of her eyes. She was seeing King Caspian pushing her on the bed, then spreading her legs and staring down at her with a mischievous smile. Her thoughts were making her weak.

"I'm so happy you're here. In a few minutes, I'm going to take you upstairs and make passionate love to you—make you scream my name and give you the best orgasm of your life. Trust me when I tell you how much I desire you, Cinderella—more than I've ever desired any other woman in my entire existence."

Chapter Six

Cindy's body tensed under his touch, and her stomach twisted in nervous knots when the king pulled away from her ear. She couldn't comprehend that he dared to say something so hot, yet outrageous to her. Inside, she knew she had never been so turned on before. Then he smiled at her while carrying her body along with the rhythm of the music, almost like they were dancing, suspended in the air. His touch was too much and yet not enough.

"And I must apologise for my son. He doesn't seem to understand that tonight he was supposed to choose a woman who could potentially be his wife. He's much too in love with himself it would seem," the king admitted, bringing Cindy back to reality from her lust-crazed state. She glanced at him, wondering if she had imagined him telling her that he wanted to make love to her. Maybe her mind was playing tricks on her.

"Yes, your son is very handsome, but I don't think any girl here is good enough for him," Cindy said, as her voice vibrated with emotion.

The king sighed loudly, like he wanted to disagree, but instead he said, "So tell me something about yourself, Cindy. Is there anyone in your life who is holding your heart captive?"

For a split second, Cindy could have sworn she saw fang-like teeth, but then she quickly dismissed the thought. Her father had talked about vampires in the past like they were real, but Cindy knew that he was only trying to scare her when she was younger. At the same time, she remembered how she got to the ball. Martha admitted that she was a changeling and then displayed her extraordinary magic. Maybe it was possible after all.

"No, there isn't. I live with my stepmother and stepsisters on the outskirts of town. My father died several years ago," she explained, and the king squeezed his long fingers around her waist a little harder. More heat rushed over her spine.

"I'm sorry to hear that, Cindy. I'm sure your father was a great man and he is terribly missed. I'm glad that he brought up such a fine-looking woman," Caspian's eyes zoomed down to her cleavage.

Cindy's heart was beating so fast that she thought it would explode in her chest at any moment. Maybe she needed to take a break and go outside for some fresh air. She had been waiting for a man like King Caspian her entire life, but was afraid to admit to herself that he was right for her. The age gap between them wasn't a problem. Charles was young and he betrayed her, maybe it was time for Cindy to focus on someone older.

"Yes, I loved him very much and I do miss him every day. Before he died, he married Ida, and she took charge of his estate. She has no idea that I'm here, you see, so I have to be careful," Cindy explained, suddenly glancing around afraid that she was going to be recognised, but thankfully her stepmother wasn't around.

The king inhaled sharply, and then brought her closer to his chest. Cindy caught the scent of his cologne. He smelled of wild forest, rain and spice. He leaned over to her ear again. "In that case, we must leave right away. I'm taking you upstairs to my private chambers. The truth is, my Cinderella, that I have wanted you since the moment I laid my eyes on you."

Now it was clear to her that she hadn't imagined him flirting with her earlier on. She didn't have a chance to form a coherent response, because the king grabbed her hand and began pulling her across the dance floor. Her thoughts were a tangled mess, and desire was burning her skin. The tiny voice in her head kept reminding her that Caspian wasn't the right man for her, but her heart disagreed.

Soon, they slipped through the tall doors, leaving the music and other guests behind. Most of the servants and other staff members bowed towards Caspian as they moved through the dark corridors farther inside the castle.

They climbed a marble staircase for several minutes, until Cindy was out of breath, finally reaching the top of the tower. Caspian looked at her and brushed his thumb over her lips as they stood outside giant, dark pine doors. A girl like Cindy didn't do things like this, and surely she wasn't prepared to sleep with a man that she'd just met. However, the slow and steady throbbing between her legs was making her reconsider her own rules.

"Tell me, Cindy, do you want to be invited inside or would you rather go back to the ball?" Caspian asked her in a serious tone.

She hated that he was making her choose, but refused to listen to the voice of reason. In a way she wanted to be seduced by an older man like the king. She didn't even care that he was royal, it no longer mattered.

Her already-pounding heart skyrocketed.

"Yes, I do," she said with a confident voice, and Caspian's eyes filled with blazing fire. He took the key and opened the door to his chamber. Cindy walked inside, mesmerised by the entire space. The room was designed in great taste. There was a large fire burning away, and two comfortable sofas were situated right in front of it. Further down Cindy noticed a huge four-poster bed in the middle of the room, with colourful cashmere throws. An image of the king kissing her flashed in front of her eyes and she felt herself blushing. Martha mentioned that she had until midnight, then her magic would fade away, but Cindy wasn't worried. She still had a few hours.

"This room is beautiful and I feel so privileged being invited to your chamber," she said, admiring his collection of paintings on the walls.

"I'm glad to hear it. Come, sit down, Cindy, let me get you a glass of wine," Caspian said, and led her to the purple sofa.

Cindy smoothed her blond hair carefully, attempting not to mess it up, trying anything to ignore the fact that she was completely aroused. She kept glancing over at the king, noticing that despite his age, he appeared to be in excellent shape. If the hard, muscular chest she had bumped into earlier was any indication of what was underneath his clothes, she definitely had something to look forward to. She couldn't wait to run her hands all over him. He stole her breath away, and his pale complexion only added more enigma to his look.

"Thank you," she said, and accepted a glass of wine from him. He kept looking at her intensely, as if he was trying to reach into the deepest parts of her soul. She wondered if he often invited other women for a private chat to his room.

"You must know that you're the only woman that I care about right now. I haven't officially been seen with anyone since Eric's mother passed away," the king explained, as if he'd just read her mind. Cindy parted her lips, but she wasn't able to respond. Her emotions were overwhelming.

Then she glanced briefly at the table and noticed an old book underneath a few others, the cover was a little damaged, but she couldn't have missed the title. It was a story about a cursed prince and the woman of his dreams. Her father used to read it to her all the time when she was younger. Cindy often imagined herself being Ellena–the woman that the young prince had fallen for.

"This book, The Broken Curse, it's one of my favourite tales of all time. I grew up believing that Tristan and Ellena were real," she said all of a sudden, quite shocked that the king was interested in that sort of literature.

Caspian looked a little stunned and then stroked his chin, not taking his eyes off of her.

"You may not believe it, but it's a book that I always carry with me. I've read it more than a hundred times. Not many men could admit liking that sort of thing, but I believe that Tristan and Ellena's romance is very inspiring. And the writing is truly exceptional. I enjoy it very much," he stated, sounding surprised too. Cindy smiled, and more warmth jolted through her heart.

She liked the fact that she and the king had something so significant in common. This book was near and dear to her heart and she wanted to think that over time Caspian might be too.

As he stood by her, tension uncoiled and Cindy held her breath for a long moment, unable to stop staring at him. Heat was radiating throughout her body, making it difficult to function, let alone speak, and she began to felt dizzy again.

Soon she forgot about the book and thought that she wanted a man who could take full control in the bedroom. A man who would dominate her and take her to the moon and back. After all, she had no experience with men and wanted her first time to be special. She didn't want to fumble around. Her stepsisters often talked about their sexual adventures and she wondered what it be like to be with a man like Caspian. She had always wanted to wait to give her virtue away to a man she loved, but she was beginning to rethink her decision and just go with it. Cindy had never met a man like Caspian before and the feelings she was experiencing in his presence were out of this world. Now she had the perfect opportunity to find out, and Caspian assured her a few times that he would please her.

The king narrowed his eyes and took off his jacket. Cindy could have sworn that she saw his skin shimmer in the dim light. Then he sat beside her, brushing his thigh against hers. She needed and wanted more.

"Tell me, Cindy, do you want me to make love to you?" he asked, like his question was perfectly normal, and then ran his finger over her bare arm. She gasped for air, and goose pimples broke out over the line where his finger had just touched her. She was staring at him, knowing that there was something different about him. The heat that she felt in his presence turned on full force, and the moment while he just sat there waiting was agonising. Cindy squeezed her legs together, aware that her panties were soaked through.

The king flexed his muscles and Cindy swallowed hard, wondering how it would feel if she kissed him. She told herself off inside of her head, because she wasn't supposed to be that kind of girl. But she didn't want to say no to him—she truly wanted him..

"Don't be afraid, darling. You're beautiful and you've been denied the pleasure of sensual lovemaking for too long. I can show you what sex is all about and you'll enjoy it, more than you can even imagine," he assured her once again.

She was done with words, so she grabbed his face and pressed her lips to his. The king seemed astonished at first, but he went with her rhythm. Their lips touched, and Cindy's body turned into a smoking flame.

His lips were confident and firm, driving the tempo, stealing her breath away. She had no idea why she nearly jumped on him, but the desire inside her clogged her mind. He slipped his tongue inside her mouth and pushed her down to the sofa, so she was underneath him. Cindy was lost in his touch, as he pressed his strong body down upon hers. She had never been kissed like that. Caspian wanted her and he sent a strong buzz down to her lady parts. He bit her lower lip then came back for more, devouring her and she was slowly losing her mind.

Then he was kissing her neck, biting slowly until she was moaning loudly. His hands were everywhere, touching her arms, then sliding his fingers underneath her dress. She could feel his length pressed against her thigh; it was driving her mad with desire.

The tiny voice in her head reminded her that she needed to stop thinking about the consequences. She pulled him deeper, wanting to feel him in every part of her mouth. Cindy rolled her hips against his, begging to be touched and ease the ache in her core.

"You fucking want me. I want you to beg me to make love to you," he rasped, finally pulling away. Cindy's body was drenched, and the throbbing between her legs was unbearable now. Her mouth felt empty and cold as she struggled for breath.

She was staring at him unable to make a decision. She couldn't imagine telling a stranger to fuck her.

Caspian's eyes flickered in the corners and he grabbed her wrists. Cindy knew that nothing was going to happen until she obeyed him.

"Yes, I want you to fuck me, please. It's the only thing that I can think about right now," she whispered, and her voice vibrated. Caspian smiled with satisfaction and then he pushed himself back, dragging her with him. She realised that the zipper in her dress was open, and her boobs were exposed. The king's eyes were filled with need and Cindy sensed that he was ready to tear the rest of her dress to pieces if she didn't hurry.

"Good girl and a good answer," he said, taking her hand as they both got up from the couch. Moments later he led her to the bed, smiling mystically. Cindy was a little nervous but tried not to show it. Her desire for this man had made her crazy, but she wasn't sure if she would even know what to do. "Don't worry about anything, just relax, because you're about to experience a night that you'll never forget."

The bedroom was filled with his cologne. The king started unbuttoning his shirt as she tried to calm her erratic breathing.

"I need to get back home before my stepmother realises that I disobeyed her," she said.

"Forget about them, and start taking your clothes off. This is our moment," he ordered, and his demanding voice caused her insides to melt. He lay on the bed and Cindy stopped acting like she was shy. It was her night, and he was the king. Her stepsisters would die from jealousy if they realised what was about to happen.

She bit her lip and moved her hips, taking her dress off very slowly at the same time. Pulsing heat was sliding down her breast and into her stomach until it curled her toes. The king widened his eyes and with a sharp intake of breath, shifted on the bed.

Cindy let her dress fall to her feet. She walked out of it and then stood in front of him wearing only her pink underwear with stockings that one of the other hookers had picked up for her.

Cindy was blessed with fair-sized boobs and she liked that the king was staring at her every move like a wolf ready to attack his prey. She ran her hand down her stomach and then slipped her fingers underneath her panties, going further than she intended.

"You have no idea how fucking sexy you look right now," the king growled, and Cindy touched her sex, feeling moist and wet. She closed her eyes and started circling her finger over her clit.

"No, this isn't how I want it. Come here, Cinderella," Caspian growled, and then pulled her to him. Cindy gasped, feeling hot everywhere. He turned her around so she was facing the wall. "Right, I'm going to make you come hard, and I want you to scream if you have to. Say 'I understand you, Your Highness'?"

"I understand you, Your Highness."

Chapter Seven

Cindy's body was responding to Caspian's commands before her brain could decide to. He was brushing his finger over her backside and she couldn't stand still. She always believed that this moment was going to be special, but she never thought that the man would be so sensual.

Caspian kicked her legs apart with his foot and caressed her arse cheeks. She closed her eyes when he settled himself between her legs. Cindy felt his enormous erection pressed over her quivering entrance.

"You smell divine, and you're so wet and ready for me," he whispered in her ear and then unhooked her bra.

She gasped for breath when his cold fingers started caressing her hardened nipples. He was incredibly hot and savage in the way he was touching her, and she knew that it wouldn't be long before she would be climaxing, screaming his name. He continued to pinch her nipple, before pulling her panties down. Her bra fell to the floor and she stepped out of her panties, realising that she was standing completely naked in front of him.

"Stunning, and all mine to play with. Do you even realise how happy it makes me to know you haven't been with any other man before?" he whispered directly into her ear.

She felt herself going red, knowing she had been waiting all her life for a man like Caspian. Now she didn't care that he was much older than her, she just wanted him to make love to her.

Cindy was surprised when he stopped teasing her altogether and instead of touching her, he pushed her directly to the bed.

"Lie down, I changed my mind. I can fuck you from behind later, baby," he commanded and Cindy obeyed him again without a word. She was getting wetter every time he ordered her to do something.

Caspian's eyes were filled with passion and greed, and Cindy's heart stopped in her chest when he lowered himself down. He was bare chested and Cindy had no idea how a man his age could have such defined muscles. His skin was pale, but she didn't have a chance to think about what was going to happen, when he pressed his lips to hers. He kissed her hard, rough, almost hurting her lips; her whole body melted underneath his strong chest.

The buzzing in her ears reminded her about the ball and Prince Eric, but as soon as Caspian started moving down she was lost in unbelievable sensations that shook through her core.

"Remember what you promised, Cindy? You have to scream. I guarantee you'll enjoy this." His voice reached her as he began showering her with kisses, moving further and further down, exploring every inch of her body with his wet, sensual tongue. She couldn't think straight, moaning when he spread her legs wide. It was the most intimate moment of her life, and the slow pulses between her legs were making her crazy. He started rubbing her clit in a slow circular motion, blowing hot breath over her as he slipped his long finger inside her core. "You're wet, so wet and only for me. Part of me wants to forget that I'm a gentlemen and just take you right now."

She had no idea what he was going to do next, but her thighs trembled with anticipation. When she finally felt his tongue on her sex, she thought that she was going to come at any moment. She wanted to beg him to touch her there over and over, to ease the ache in her core. Cindy felt the pressure that was building up in the lower part of her stomach, wondering why she hadn't tried having sex sooner.

The moment he started to lick her up and down she knew she wasn't going to last long. Every part of her body was on fire, and her heart pounded in her chest. She was taking air into her lungs, but she felt drunk on desire.

Caspian was riding her with his tongue, and she was moaning loudly ready to break apart and experience her first real orgasm.

His skilled fingers fucked her, plunging in and pulling out in fast, steady strokes as he sucked and licked her sex. She clenched the silky sheets on the bed as she felt her orgasm climbing to its peak.

Moments later, he stopped and she cried out from the loss of contact. Then he stuck his forefinger inside of her. This was all too much for Cindy, because all the sensations that she began to experience were making her dizzy. She was gasping for breath, and her chest kept rising and falling repeatedly.

The king lowered himself down and continued licking her. She moaned loudly, as her muscles tightened and her core clenched around his finger. Small beads of sweat rolled down her face.

"You're so close, so damn close and I'm looking forward to seeing you come for me. I want you to come on my face," the king whispered, and kept moving his finger in and out.

Then her whole body went rigid as he was still caressing her tender nerves with his tongue with endless devotion. Cindy's body exploded with ecstasy, and she experienced the most intense orgasm of her lifetime. She clenched her fingers around the sheets so hard that she cut off her blood circulation, and screamed his name over and over. Her body convulsed with fire for several heartbeats until she was just lying on the bed, experiencing the buzzing after-warmth of nerves in every part of her numb body. When her vision and then her mind cleared, Cindy found Caspian holding her closely.

"Just hold on. That was the most beautiful thing that I've ever seen, and soon I'll be coming with you."

Cindy was unable to respond, as she felt him standing up. When she glanced up at him, she saw him taking off the rest of his clothes. She thought that he looked so handsome in the dim candlelight, broad, muscular and just perfect.

"Now, we're going to make love. You're so ready and you don't have to worry about anything. I will be gentle," he told her and she giggled to herself, not believing that this was really happening. Her hands were shaking, and her heart was still beating loudly in her chest.

"Your eyes and skin," she whispered more to herself than him, seeing that the king's eyes were shimmering like diamonds, but soon he moved on top of her, and once he pressed his lips to hers she'd forgotten all about it.

She was melting yet again beneath his magnificent body, lost in the electrifying touch of his lips. He cupped her breasts and ran his hand down to her hips, and continued kissing her at the same time. Cindy was a little afraid of the fact that she was still a virgin, and clenched her palm over his strong muscles, digging her nails into his skin. She dragged her hand through his thick hair and then felt his hard erection between her legs. He was huge and she moaned loudly, thinking that maybe he wouldn't fit inside her. The king must have sensed her hesitation, because he looked at her.

"Don't worry, you're wet and ready. You will love it when I'm inside you," he told her and spread her legs wider. Caspian aligned his erection with her opening and entered her slowly, only partway, giving her time to adjust to his size.

She gasped when he filled her up and felt his full length. Cindy arched her head backward, experiencing the pain. She tried to breathe at the same time, wanting it all to stop. The pain soon turned into a slight discomfort. Her pulse was racing away and she needed to ease the need of being with this gorgeous man.

She tried to ignore the pain while he invaded her with his size, then slowly he began moving inside her.

"Look at me, Cindy, I want you to look at me when I'm claiming you as my own," he rasped, and she obeyed him. "You are so tight, perfect and beautiful."

Cindy was losing her head, and soon she managed to forget about the pain. The king was moving inside her and she held him close. She moaned loudly when he lifted her up to a sitting position. She couldn't remember ever feeling so completely filled, not because of his size, but because of the way his eyes pierced hers as he began to fill her in with his length. His lovemaking felt intense, and soon he was pounding into her, not holding back. She couldn't take it, and she knew that she would come again soon.

Then when she was ready to climax, he lowered his lips to her breast, and took her left nipple into his teeth. She didn't register the pain, and a jolt of pleasant pain shot through her.

"Now, let me fuck you hard. I think you're ready. Tell me that you're ready," he ordered her, and then he pulled away, abruptly turning her around so she was on all fours.

"Yes, yes master. I'm ready," she shouted and then felt him entering her from behind while caressing her arse cheeks. It was bliss and she bit her lip until it bled, knowing she was going to come again at any moment.

He was riding her hard, breathing harder and telling her to hold on for a few more seconds. She screamed, feeling him pounding his hard erection into her over and over.

Cindy felt like her body began levitating above the bed, as the king was reaching deep inside her core. He gripped her hips and then they both started coming at the same time.

She screamed loudly, mostly his name as the heat filled her. Her heart pounded as he came inside her. Soon enough, they both collapsed on top of each other, their breathing laboured.

Caspian was caressing her back, moving his fingers up and down. Cindy melted, trying to understand what had just happened between them. She didn't know anything about this enigmatic man, and yet she let him touch her very soul, reaching further than anyone ever had. Her stepmother could go to hell and take the narcissistic prince with her too. The sex with the king, her first time, made her feel alive. Maybe in the past she felt the same way about the forest ranger, but now what happened back at the tavern was a distance memory.

Her lip was still bleeding a little, but she didn't care. Her body felt so relaxed and she was ready to give her heart away to the king. He was the man that she'd been waiting for this entire time.

"This was amazing; you were right. I was silly to be so scared," she admitted and then turned to face him. In that moment she didn't care that she was still naked in front of him. For years she worried about her body, but now it didn't matter. She felt a drop of blood escaping from the corner of her mouth. The king moved beneath her, his eyes widened, and then he licked his lips.

"Blood. You must have cut yourself," he whispered, and then Cindy saw that Caspian didn't have normal teeth. Instead he had real fangs. Fear paralysed her to the core, because she was certain that she was staring at a creature who wasn't supposed to exist.

Vampire: that was the first thing that came to her mind. She remembered seeing his skin shimmering, almost glowing, and she could have sworn that she saw his fangs earlier too. Her father talked about very pale creatures that drank blood from humans, like he believed that vampires truly existed.

"You're a vampire.... No, no, no this can't be happening," she whispered quickly backing away from him. Her thoughts were racing all of a sudden, but she was still lucid enough to start picking up her clothes.

She managed to dress herself with enormous speed, mumbling words that didn't make any sense. The king was staring at her and Cindy felt ashamed and frightened that he might have placed some kind of charm on her.

"Yes, Cindy, you've learned my secret. I'm a vampire, but that doesn't change anything. We're into each other, and you gave yourself to me fully tonight. The blood, I would have never tried drinking from you without your permission. Please stay, so I can explain everything properly," the king said, trying to locate his own pants, but Cindy kept shaking her head.

She swallowed past the lump of fear growing in her throat. She couldn't comprehend how she didn't notice earlier that the king wasn't human. This couldn't be true, he was the King of Farrington Kingdom and just a few minutes ago he gave her one of the most amazing orgasms and took her virginity.

He jumped off the bed, standing in front of her naked and pale. Now she was seeing through him, realising that she had made the biggest mistake of her life. He must have glamoured her in order to persuade her to his chamber, to make her his.

"No, I don't want anything to do with you. This didn't happen and I wasn't even here!" she shouted and then flew across the room, barging through the door. And once she was outside the king's chamber, she started running, remembering that she'd forgotten her panties.

Chapter Eight

The king stood in his chamber completely naked and furious. He kept asking himself how the hell he let the woman of his dreams run away like that. There was something wrong with him. His normally sharp mind wasn't working the way it was supposed to. Well, he knew exactly why; he just had the best sex of his life and yet he let the girl go.

Caspian had a chance to get to know her before the ball. They met at the market for the first time and that morning everything could have easily turned against him— because Cindy knew the man from whom Caspian had borrowed the identity from. Luckily, some other man apologised to her, using her name, so the King could carry on pretending to be the forest ranger. He was surprised and smitten at the same time. He often turned into some random human men, that way he could leave the castle undetected and undisturbed. The king instantly thought that Cindy was sweet, innocent and reminded him a lot of his dead wife, Catherine. He was lost in a swirl of desire and the need to sink his fangs into her neck.

They talked for hours, and it was clear to the King that Cindy held some sort of crush on Charles. She was shy, innocent, and yet she had a big heart. Caspian didn't like that he had to lie to her about his identity, so he carried on meeting her as Charles. It seemed to him that Cindy didn't have a lot of freedom, and her stepmother was forcing her to do all the chores around the house. Every time they parted ways he couldn't stop thinking about her, and he didn't even care that she was much younger.

Then finally one night she waited for him in local Tavern, and he couldn't believe his own luck. He only wanted her for himself, so they walked around the forest, then started fooling around.

Caspian was shocked to learn that Cindy was a virgin. He forgot about her blood, and focused on his desire. She was so responsive, and for a moment he had forgotten that they were in the forest. Caspian wanted her first time to be spectacular, but then they were caught by her stepmother. Everything happened so fast, and a split second later she was gone. The King was lost in a need of sinking his fangs into her neck.

Furious and still hungry he returned to the castle, unable to stop thinking about her erotic scent and pure soul. She never took him to her home, but he knew he could track her down somehow. Instead, he decided to wait until after the ball.

He dragged his hand through his hair and swore a few times, realising that he should have pursued her much sooner, but at the same time he was afraid of rejection. He was thirsty for her tantalising blood, a growing need raging deep inside him, and on top of that, he was still hard. Several minutes later, he put on his dressing robe and barged out of his chamber.

Cindy couldn't get far; the ball downstairs was still going on and he just needed to talk to her. Humans were always afraid of the truth, but once they understood that vampires were very similar, they calmed down.

"Guards, guards!" he called out, storming through the dark corridors, trying to tame the ongoing desire that was boiling in his blood. No one in the castle knew that he was a so-called, bloodsucking monster who hunted humans after dark. He'd managed to keep that secret for years, but tonight Cindy had seen past his glamour. Caspian had let his guard down, because he felt connected to her. She practically flew out of his chamber and he just stood there, not even trying to stop her.

"My lord, my lord, what happened?" one of the guards asked, approaching. There were two others right behind him, looking alert.

"A young blond woman just left my chamber. She can't be far. I want you to stop her. I need to speak to her urgently," the king ordered, ready to use his supernatural abilities to track her down, but it was too much of a risk. There were too many people in the castle tonight and the king needed to be careful. The guards were loyal to him and never asked any questions.

He didn't even taste her blood, but he was already craving it. Cinderella's scent was enticing, and it consumed his mind. It took him a moment to realise that he was only in his robe, so he quickly returned to his chamber to change. Then he saw something on the floor by the bed, something that didn't belong to him.

Caspian liked sleeping with human women, but since his son came of the age, he hadn't been with anyone for years. In the past, he was out on the town almost every night, obviously with a concealed identity.

"Cindy, my hot, needy Cindy. It looks like you left me a souvenir," he muttered to himself, picking up her pink lace knickers that made him want to fuck her again. His cock stirred in his pants when he picked them up and inhaled her scent. The king had never lost control like that, but tonight he'd forgotten about his own rules. Cindy was the most beautiful creature that he'd ever laid eyes on. In the past, he used his glamour to make other mortals forget that they'd ever met him. He thought that he would sleep with Cindy and then forget about her, but now he knew it would be impossible. He'd lost his mind for her.

Caspian found some decent clothes in his closet and put them on, shaking his head at the same time. For the first time since his Catherine had passed away, he truly desired another woman. But the fact that his kind fed on blood frightened her, which was understandable.

They had an instant connection and Caspian was impressed that Cindy was so humble and innocent. He was elated to learn that she had never been with any other man—a virgin—and all his to explore for the first time. He enjoyed taking control, showing her what he was capable of. Several moments later, someone knocked on his chamber door. He sighed loudly, sensing that Malcom had returned without Cindy. She must have gotten away.

"There is no sign of her anywhere my lord, all the guards have been looking everywhere. The ball is still going and your —"

"What is the meaning of this, Father? I've been searching for you for over half an hour now," Eric interrupted Malcolm, suddenly appearing in the corridor. Caspian raised both his eyebrows, seeing that his son wasn't alone. A very ugly human girl was standing behind him, glancing around. Normally Caspian wouldn't pay attention to the fact that his son chose to spend time with someone that wasn't very attractive. He believed that beauty came from the inside, not the outside, but his son had a particular taste in women. The king had to admit that Eric was shallow and his arrogance was beyond annoying. For years, he had been telling everyone that once he settled down, he wouldn't go for any ordinary girl—unless she had royal blood in her veins.

"Eric, you should be entertaining your guests at the ball. We can talk about whatever this is later. I'm kind of busy right now," the king explained, wondering if he made a mistake bringing the guards into his search for Cindy.

"The guests downstairs have food, drinks and music. They're fine. I've finally chosen the woman that I'm ready to spend the rest of my life with. Let me introduce you to Rigga. She's from Desmout Kingdom. Her father is the Governor," Eric said, sounding very proud of himself.

After months of preparation and planning, the ball was finally happening, but right now the king no longer cared that his son had finally decided to pull his head from his backside.

Caspian didn't like to judge, but Rigga was very pale, she had short black hair, a square, very masculine jaw and carried a bit of weight too. Eric was much too blinded by his own ego and it seemed that he had chosen Rigga, because he wanted to get Caspian off his back. The King had been telling himself for years that his son wasn't one of the brightest of men in the kingdom, and he had tried hard to sharpen his mind by educating him the best way he knew how, but to no avail. Tonight Eric had proven to him that he was still very much the immature prince, but at least he had chosen his future wife. Maybe Rigga would lead him to be great—Caspian just needed to have more faith in him.

Unfortunately, he was done babysitting him, and needed to find Cindy.

"I'm glad and it's truly an honour to meet you, Rigga," Caspian stated, sounding annoyed. "Please, both of you go back to the ballroom. I need to take care of something."

The girl smiled shyly at him, and went instantly red. The prince looked angry, but he didn't say anything when the king moved past him. As soon as he was alone, he felt thirsty again, and for some reason the craving for Cindy's blood burned his throat. His cock was semi hard, and he kept having sexual flashbacks about his time with Cindy.

Heat blossomed throughout his body as he continued moving downstairs, hoping that his guards were going to be able to locate the woman of his dreams.

He married Catherine, Eric's mother, almost twenty years ago. They loved each other very much and she never cared that he was a vampire. Of course he told her the truth from the beginning, and she accepted his terms. Unfortunately, she passed away during childbirth and he couldn't save her then. His blood had healing properties, but she was already on the other side, and fate had taken her away from him.

He wasn't prepared to turn her into a vampire, because he didn't want that kind of life for her. Catherine had a pure soul, and that's why he'd fallen in love with her in the first place. When he lost her, his whole world had fallen to pieces; he locked himself in his chamber for months afterwards, not wanting to go on living.

His advisors ruled his kingdom until he was ready to return. He had Eric and knew he had to take care of him, for Catherine. People respected him and he looked after them well. He didn't care for any other woman; his grief made him immune to love...until he saw Cindy at the ball. Something sparked inside of him when he saw her standing across the room—something he hadn't felt in over twenty years.

Years later, when Eric got older, Caspian began leaving the castle, using his glamour to conceal his true identity from humans. It was almost fifteen years after he had lost his beloved Catherine. It took him that long to even consider sleeping with other women. In the beginning, he was only having fun, but then he began feeding off of lonely peasants, lords, and even hunters. If he ever slept with a woman he always made sure that they didn't remember what had happened, then returned to the castle. But there was always something missing.

Eric grew up to be a brave man, but even Caspian had to admit that he was much too in love with himself. The king had no idea who he inherited that kind of character trait from. Neither he nor his mother were ever that vain. Years went by and soon enough it was clear to Caspian that Eric wasn't going to be the right kind of king for Farrington unless he got married. The king believed that his son could be guided by a smart, beautiful and decent woman, like he had been when Catherine was still alive.

He set to organise the ball, and sent his advisors around to deliver the invitations to all the available ladies in the Farrington Kingdom. Many people in the castle believed that Eric wasn't ready to settle down, but Caspian was done waiting around. The king was even considering using his glamour to put Eric back on the right path. He walked around the dance floor, watching his son wasting this opportunity, making an absolute fool of himself, yet again. He was surrounded by beautiful women, and they all wanted him to notice them, but instead he chose to talk about himself and his good looks.

Then he bumped into Cindy again on the dance floor, and in that moment he stopped worrying about Eric. He just couldn't believe that she would show up, and she was alone too. He recognised her instantly, he had been dreaming about her scent and body for days since her stepmother caught them in the bushes. He couldn't tell her the truth, so he carried on with his act. He was afraid that she would ran away or hate him forever.

"Nothing, my lord, we've checked everywhere. She must have been in the carriage that just left from the back gate," one of the guards announced, pulling him away from his long-winded thoughts. It seemed that the guard ran all the way to tell him the bad news, because he was struggling to catch his breath.

Caspian clenched his fists, telling himself that he had to stay calm. Cindy couldn't live far from the castle, and he could look for her tomorrow. He'd forgotten about his glamour after they made love, and she noticed his fangs. Catherine was afraid of him in the beginning too, but after some time she came around. He just had to hope that eventually Cindy would let him explain everything.

For the first time he believed that he had finally found a woman who could replace his Catherine.

"All right, just keep looking. I'm taking Storm for a ride," he announced, not wanting to sound too desperate. The guard nodded and walked away.

He shook his head and then returned to his chamber, knowing that he should be at the ball, taking care of his royal duties. He had invited a few important guests and really needed to at least make an appearance.

The problem was that the king couldn't focus. Cindy's scent was all over his bed, and he kept imagining having her in his arms. She wanted him. Maybe she was a little afraid that he was older and much more experienced, but she had given herself away to him fully and completely. He thought that he would go crazy if he stayed in his chamber a moment longer, so after some time he decided to go back to the ball. When he got there, Eric was on the dance floor with Rigga. Most of the ladies looked disappointed, and a few were crying.

Caspian sighed loudly and began walking around, hoping to find someone who could tell him something more about the mysterious Cindy. He even considered going back to the tavern. He was sure that someone was bound to know her there because she was a local. She lived with her stepmother and two stepsisters, and that her father died when she was thirteen.

"It was a waste of time coming here, Susan. The prince didn't even look at you or your sister once. It's a complete disgrace that he humiliated everyone here by dancing on his own," said an older woman, possibly in her late forties or early fifties, dressed in a blue sparkly dress as she passed Caspian. She was fanning herself with a small fan and looked like someone who was born to a good family.

"At least we had fun," admitted the young ginger girl, most likely her daughter, who then whispered to the other girl that was walking next to her. "And I met a few barons. They're going to visit me in the fall."

They both giggled, and the woman gave them a stern look.

"The older baron and I had fun in the back of his carriage. This party was awesome enough, but yeah, the prince is a moron. Did you see the girl that he eventually picked? Yuck," the blond girl said. Caspian smiled to himself, thinking about the older obese baron he had invited to the ball. He had a double chin and was half his height. At least some of the girls knew how to enjoy themselves.

But the King was frustrated, and that was an understatement. He needed to speak to Cindy right away. He clenched his teeth, staring as the woman and her two daughters were leaving. A few other guests were departing as well.

He knew the moment he saw her at the market that she could replace his Catherine. Right now he was willing to do anything to find her and explain everything. He didn't care that he was older than her and she was below his social class—Cindy had to be his again. Ideally forever.

Chapter Nine

Somehow Cindy managed to find her magical carriage and get outside the castle gate before the clock struck midnight. She was sitting inside, trying to calm her laboured breathing, thinking about her first time with a man and how it couldn't have been better. The king made her feel special, and he took care of her needs like a real gentleman. The fire inside her kept burning and she couldn't stop thinking about his demanding voice.

Vampire. She kept reminding herself that he was a monster, and if she hadn't run out of there, he could have attacked her, drank her blood or even killed her. She felt stupid that she didn't put the obvious signs together much sooner, but she was so blinded by her unexpected desire that she chose to ignore them. None of this was acceptable, yet she couldn't stop thinking about the way he made her feel.

Cindy had wondered about her first time with a man often, but she never thought the sexual act itself could be so incredibly satisfying. Caspian was gentle, yet demanding and intense. She still had goosebumps all over her body remembering what he had whispered in her ear at the ball.

She glanced out the window of her carriage, seeing the bright castle in the distance. Her fingers were trembling and she was ready to tell the coachman to turn around. A few deep breaths later, she sat back in the carriage, shaking her head and trying to reason with herself.

Maybe for a few hours she had lost her head, but she never thought that the king would be so handsome or that he was a vampire. It was a nightmare; there was no way that she could trust him again. She needed to hide, and forget that he ever existed. Her heart rate was picking up again, and her palms were damp with sweat. She arched her head backwards and began breathing steadily, but nothing was helping. Cindy just couldn't stop thinking about the way Caspian made her feel—alive and in control.

She had no idea what time it was, but Cindy hoped that her stepmother and stepsisters hadn't returned home before her. The ball would go on for another few hours, but she had no idea how long she had been with the king. He must have used some kind of charm or illusion once she agreed to spend the night in his chamber, but even thinking past that, she still wanted him.

The carriage stopped abruptly and the horses jolted. Cindy had no idea where she was and realised that she was still far away from home, now surrounded by pitch-black darkness. Fear cooled the heat pooling inside of her, reminding her of the ever-growing anxiety of being alone in the dark.

She couldn't keep sitting in the carriage, so she forced herself to step outside to see what was going on, still wearing her silver heels and the amazing red dress that Martha gifted to her earlier.

"What's going on? Why have we stopped?" she asked, looking at the handsome coachman that in theory was still only a beggar that the hooker picked up from the street.

The coachman stood up, dropped his whip and all of a sudden his eyes rolled to the back of his head. Seconds later, he started spinning around and then fell to the ground, turning back into a filthy, long-haired beggar. The same thing happened with the two beautiful white horses. Martha's magic only worked until midnight, and now Cindy found herself standing in front of the old trolley that Martha had used to create her carriage. Her dream burst like a bubble and her worst nightmare was slowly turning into a reality. She was stuck in the middle of the road, alone in the dark.

She glanced down at her beautiful dress and shoes, wondering how she would get home now. The beggars were scratching their heads in confusion, glancing at each other, then back at her. She needed to pinch herself. Maybe the entire night was only a dream, and soon she would wake up.

Moments later, the beggars started running towards the forest, and Cindy assumed they were done standing around and went looking for shelter. Heavy stones of nausea cascaded down to her stomach and she swallowed the lump of fear in her throat, looking around anxiously. She wanted to curl up under a tree and stay there until morning, but deep down she knew she couldn't. She had to get back to the house, even if that meant that she had to walk back in the dark. Lost and slightly aggravated that Martha's charms had faded away so suddenly, she lifted her dress and started walking in the direction she thought her house would be.

A fine sheet of cold sweat peppered her forehead and gut-wrenching fear settled low in her stomach. It was so dark, even the moon disappeared behind the heavy clouds. Cindy forced herself to walk one foot in front of the other, knowing well enough that soon her stepmother's carriage might be passing by.

She had no idea how, but she'd found her way—a couple hours later, she was safe at home. The fear of being caught by Ida forced her to keep on going, and in a way she'd conquered her fear of the darkness. Once she reached the house, she took off her heels; she had blisters all over her feet and was extremely exhausted. There was no way in hell she would do something like that again. Upstairs in her room, she started to undress. She struggled with the zipper, and after about ten minutes, she finally placed her ball dress on the chair, and when Cindy looked down, she realised that she was missing her lace panties. Heat rushed to her face as she remembered that she had left them in the castle.

"Unbelievable," she whispered to herself and then giggled, remembering the king's head between her legs. She shuddered with excitement, knowing that he literally made her come only using his fingers. She was getting wet again just thinking about it.

Then a noise from outside brought her back to reality. She ran to the window and saw her stepmother's carriage, the same one that used to belong to her papa, arriving back outside the house. Cindy quickly switched off the lamps, knowing that her stepmother wouldn't hesitate to check on her if she noticed the lights in the windows. She'd hidden the dress in her wardrobe, just in case; she knew that her stepmother never looked in there.

For a moment, she watched how both her stepsisters and stepmother headed over to the house. Teresa was complaining that her shoes were too small and Susan was moaning that she was tired. Cindy put her nightgown on and went to bed after everyone disappeared inside the house. She wanted to forget about the night with the king and the fact that he was a vampire. She knew that their relationship could never work, and she had no idea what had gotten into her a few hours earlier, but her mind was in turmoil.

Unfortunately, she couldn't fall asleep. She was still turned on and couldn't stop imagining herself in Caspian's huge bed. His scent was still all over her body, and her nipples hardened as she remembered him touching her in the most intimate way. She ended up tossing and turning for several hours afterwards.

At some point, probably in the early hours of the morning, she finally managed to drift away, still remembering the king's electrifying touch on her body. It was bliss, but she knew that she had to forget about it as soon as possible, because she would never marry a vampire, even if he was a king.

But she still had her memories.

**

"Get up, Cindy, get up. Mommy has been calling you for ages!"

Cindy opened her eyes and saw Teresa standing in her room by her bed. She rubbed her eyes lifting herself up, barely remembering the night before. It was unusual for her to see her stepsister in her attic room. Cindy must have slept in this morning.

"What? What time it is?" she mumbled, feeling tired. She was tossing and turning all night, so she only had a few hours of sleep.

"It's ten o'clock and you were supposed to be up ages ago. All the animals need feeding and Mommy wants you to run to town to get her dress and groceries. Get a move on," Teresa ordered and Cindy suddenly remembered everything that went on last night. Her body was pleasantly numb when she thought about the king, and she giggled to herself.

"All right, all right. I'm up now," she said.

"Hurry up, you lazy cow; otherwise you'll be in big trouble," her stepsister snapped and then marched out of the room. Cindy heard her heavy footsteps all the way downstairs—she stomped like a herd of buffalos.

Cindy lay back down, breathing steadily and thinking about her night with the king. Five minutes later, she was putting her clothes on, not wanting to anger her stepmother even more. It looked like no one had noticed that she was gone most of the night. Ida most likely thought that she had been sulking in her room, and Cindy wasn't planning to say anything about Caspian.

Later on, after her stepmother told her off about sleeping through midmorning, she gave Cindy a list of things that she wanted her to do for the day, then sent her off to town to run some errands. It was late and Cindy knew that she would most likely be working until midnight in order to catch up.

Small beads of sweat were running down her back as she walked down the road toward the market. Last night with the king messed her up, but thankfully he had no idea who she really was—he only knew her first name. Despite her mixed feelings, she was hoping that he would never find her. It was better for her that she stay away from the vampire and his castle.

Half an hour later, she was at the market, doing a bit of grocery shopping. Earlier on, her stepmother had mentioned that she was expecting some guests for dinner tonight and she wanted Cindy to help out in the kitchen. The temperature was rising fast and she wasn't looking forward to working today.

The bags were heavy and she was still exhausted from night before. Then halfway home one of her bags split and all the groceries fell to the ground. Cindy cursed in anger and then flopped on the ground feeling miserable. She'd had enough and was ready to spend a night away from home. Nothing was going her way today, and on top of everything, she still hadn't confronted her stepmother about Londis. Ida was going through with her plan, and Cindy couldn't just wait around and do nothing. She had to act, and fast.

"Hey, are you all right?" asked a voice to her right. Cindy lifted her head, seeing Red Riding Hood standing on the road. She had a basket in her hand and was smiling at Cindy.

"No, everything is falling apart," Cindy responded, wanting to tell her everything that had happened in the past several days. She knew that it wasn't a good idea, but Cindy and Red used to be friends; they had drifted apart as the years went by. They had a huge fight and stopped talking altogether. Now, neither of them could remember what that fight was about.

Red was a beautiful girl. She had long, dark curly hair, long legs and very fair skin. Her eyes were the colour of honey and gold, and she always wore a long red cloak. Now Cindy felt even more guilty about Charles. She should have told her about him much sooner.

"It looks like you need a cold drink and a friendly chat. Come on, Cindy, my house is just around the corner," Red said and reached out her hand.

"I have to go home. I have tonnes of housework to do and my step—"

"Screw your stepmother. She's the biggest twat I know. You aren't her slave and you can do what you want," Red stated and then Cindy took her hand, smiling to herself. She helped her back on her feet, and Red quickly put the ruined shopping bag in her basket.

"Well, she isn't treating me right that's for sure," Cindy admitted more to herself, knowing that she was going to be told off for being late anyway, so she might as well catch a break with Red. They hadn't spoken for years and Cindy had been ready to hook up with her boyfriend—the forest ranger. Then she remembered that she didn't care about him anymore, because the vampire king had taken control of her mind and body. She lost her head for him and couldn't even think about anyone else—her mind was a jumbled mess.

"Come on, spill it out. What's going on? You look pissed off?" Red asked, once they reached her house. Red gestured for Cindy to sit down by the table and then placed a bottle of whiskey in front of her.

The truth was that Cinderella wasn't a very big drinker, but it was one of those days. Besides, she needed a bit of liquid courage to tell Red everything that happened last night.

Cindy bit her lip and poured the golden liquid into her glass. She didn't wait for Red; she just drank it down in one go. The liquid burned her throat.

"I had sex with the vampire king last night, and I ran away when I realised who he was. And my stepmother wants to marry me off to some stupid guy that lives on a farm in the middle of nowhere," she explained, knowing that there was no point beating around the bush, might as well lay it all out there. She needed to get this off her chest and Red seemed to be trying to rekindle their friendship.

Red's eyes widened, then she laughed loudly for about fifteen seconds, shaking her mass of curly hair.

"You were never a joker, Cindy, but you're making up for it now," Red chuckled.

"I'm not joking. The king, the father of the prince, is a vampire. He seduced me last night at the ball," Cindy said, raising her voice a little. Her heart made a flip in her chest when she thought what she let the king do to her last night. She was instantly turned on again, remembering how good his hands felt on her body. Even her heart started to beat faster.

Red's eyes nearly popped out of their sockets and then she stared at her with her jaw wide open. Five minutes later, Cindy went through everything that had happened since her stepmother introduced her to Londis, the marriage and finally, the ball. Red cursed so badly that it made Cindy ashamed of her own thoughts, and then she started pacing around in her small kitchen.

Red lived in a wooden cottage that she used to share with her grandmother who recently moved out. Cindy didn't know how much Red's life changed before the two of them lost touch, but she wanted to be in her shoes—to have a life of her own. Red was living alone and no one ever told her what to do. She had her freedom.

"Fuck, Cindy, this is huge," Red stated, and then licked her bottom lip. "So the sex was that good, huh?"

Cindy shook her head, she was ready to scream that the sex was the best of her life, but that wasn't the point. She'd never dreamed sex could be that good. Red needed to understand that the entire kingdom was ruled by a vampire for the past twenty years. It wasn't fair that the people had no idea that Caspian wasn't human.

"The vampire, Red, the king is a bloodsucking monster who glamours people!" Cindy shouted and then drank some more of the golden whiskey and felt instantly drunk. She was definitely a lightweight.

Red laughed and waved her hand dismissively and lifted her boobs.

"Girl, if someone made me come like that, I wouldn't care if he was a troll. Besides, he's royal, rich and he can get you out of that marriage with the horrible farmer, Londis," Red stated, popping her hand under her chin and sighing loudly.

"How? I can't disobey my stepmother's wishes. She's going to disinherit me."

"So, let her. If you marry the king you wouldn't have to worry about any of it. You shouldn't let her treat you like a servant. It's your house and your rules. Come on, Cindy, it's time for you to stand up to her."

Chapter Ten

Cindy never liked confrontations, but Red was absolutely right. She let her stepmother rule her and treat her like crap. After her father died, she sunk into a deep depression and Ida had used her emotional state to take full control of the estate. Besides Cindy was still a child then, and even if she stood up to her stepmother, she had no idea what would happen to her.

"King Caspian isn't suitable and I can't marry him. Besides, he's like fifteen or even twenty years older than me, and a vampire. It was just sex…"

"Yes, the most amazing, thrilling and explosive sex of your life, not to mention, your first time. Who can say they lost their virginity to an incredibly hot and sexy vampire king?" Red finished for her giggling like she was going a bit crazy. Cindy sighed, knowing that her friend was right, yet again. "Man, I wish the forest ranger was like that. He's so lousy in bed."

Cindy rubbed her forehead, feeling ashamed of herself. She was a terrible friend, thinking that she could be in love with Charles once Red was done with him. It looked like everything worked out for the best. Red needed someone in her life, and Cindy was done with her crush on her now-ex-boyfriend, Charles. She wanted to fix her relationship with Red. They used to spend most of their time together, and Cindy knew that there was more to life than cleaning and cooking.

"Yes, the sex was great, but I can't keep thinking about it. I bet he has many other women in his bed. He may not even remember me anymore. Everything happened so fast," Cindy said, and bitter disappointment filled her stomach. She didn't want him to sleep with other women or forget about her. As much as she was scared, she still desired him.

"Gee, you're so lame. He was the one who picked you at the ball where there were hundreds of other girls and then he fucked you senseless. Obviously you meant something to him, Cindy," Red said, shaking her head. Cindy was still confused, but Red was making sense. The king chose her, and she couldn't deny their instant connection.

"I know, but I have to go. My stepmother may start looking for me soon."

"Oh, forget about her, she's doesn't own you and it's time to remind her that you're not her servant. Seriously, marry the vampire king, and tell that Londis guy to get lost," Red said, sounding annoyed most likely that Cindy wasn't listening. Moments later, someone was knocking on Red's front door.

"Are you expecting someone?" Cindy asked her. Red shook her head, looking a bit worried, but went to the door.

"Is this the residence of Miss…"

His voice was a little muffled, so Cindy moved closer. She peered through the curtains that separated the kitchen from the porch and saw a man outside dressed in a navy uniform that

Cindy recognised from the castle. Her heart leapt in her throat, because she knew that it was one of Caspian's guards.

"What's this about?" Red asked.

"King Caspian met a lady at the ball last night, but she ran once she learned who he was," the messenger announced, and Cindy nearly jumped with joy. Caspian didn't forget about her, and he had sent his guards to look for her. She thought it was very romantic—almost like a fairytale. Red glanced back behind her, most likely sensing that Cindy was listening in.

"Right, so how can I help you?" she asked the guard.

"The lady left her underwear in his chamber. The king sent a few of us hoping that we would find her. Her name is Cindy and he knows that she's a resident of Farrington Kingdom. The king would like to speak to her urgently," the messenger explained.

"Hold on a second," Red said and shut the door in his face before he could say another word. Red had never cared about manners. She walked into the kitchen laughing to herself.

"I told you so. The king's looking for you, and this guy must have been out since dawn, riding around with your panties in his pocket." Red continued to chuckle. "Darling, you have been a very, very naughty girl."

"Shut up and just pretend that you don't know anything. I have to go. I bet he was already at my house, talking to my stepmother. This is a complete disaster," Cindy hissed, panicking, and before Red could stop her, she barged through the back door, forgetting her shopping bags.

She ran all the way back to the house, knowing that by now her stepmother most likely already knew that she'd disobeyed her and went to the ball. She was sure that there wasn't any other girl named Cindy who lived in Farrington. Then, she remembered Red's words and slowed down a bit. Cindy had to stop being such a pushover and start speaking her mind.

She walked all the way back to the house, not hurrying anymore. She couldn't believe the king had sent his guards to look for her. He was a bloodsucking creature, but she must have made an impression on him. Either way, she decided that she needed to at least give him a chance.

"You need to calm down and just say what's on your mind. You had every right to be at the ball," she told herself, walking through the gate. That pep talked helped a little, and Cindy felt good about seeing Ida.

"Well, well, well...someone is in the huge trouble now." The voice of Susan startled her a little. She turned around spotting her stepsister by the path. "I really didn't think you had the balls, Cindy."

Teresa stood beside her, and when Cindy didn't respond they both laughed. She continued to breathe in steadily. Then, she realised that she left all her shopping bags and Ida's dress at Red's house. It didn't matter anymore. She was done taking orders from her stepmother.

"At least I found someone who wants me, and I don't have to hide it anymore," she snapped back at Susan and walked inside the house. She felt relieved and was ready to tell her stepsisters that she wasn't done with them. They were cruel to her, and she was ready to kick their arses if either of them came anywhere near her ever again. Cindy knew she had to locate the old paperwork and find out exactly what her father had written in the will. She didn't believe that he would allow Ida to choose her husband. The whole idea was absurd.

Ida was in the living room, sitting on the sofa and holding a cup of tea in her right hand. As soon as Cindy saw her, she felt a little scared, but knew she couldn't change her mind now. Besides, the whole estate was hers before Ida came into the picture—she needed to put Ida in her place. But first, Cindy just needed to find a lawyer who could help her with real estate legalities and wills.

"Sit down, Cindy, we have a lot to talk about," her stepmother ordered her, but Cindy didn't move. This was a start and Cindy needed to show her that she wasn't sacred.

Cindy wasn't an idiot, she knew what she wanted and was willing to fight for her dreams.

"No, I'm fine standing. It's about time we talk about the way you've been treating me. We aren't family and you can't tell me what to do. I'm twenty years old, and this house belongs to me. My father left it to me as an inheritance and you're the one living here as a guest, stepmother," she said, more firmly than she intended, placing her hands on her hips.

She thought that it was a good start, and Cindy wasn't even planning to stop. She needed to set her own rules. Her stepmother was a stern woman, and over the years, Cindy learned that Ida liked manipulating people. She managed to seduce her father, and within a week she had him wrapped around her little finger.

The older woman narrowed her eyes at Cindy, and her cheeks went slightly pink.

"You disobeyed my order and went to the ball after I forbid you to leave this house. Then humiliated yourself and this family by sleeping with the king. I'm disgusted with your behaviour. I thought that your father had brought you up better than this. He asked me to make him a promise before he died. He wanted to see you happy, and I was supposed to match you with the right man. Mr. Londis is the perfect candidate. I have no idea what you've been thinking, but the king of this kingdom would never choose you as his life companion or wife," Cindy's stepmother stated, not even taking a breath during her entire speech.

Cindy wanted to roll her eyes, but she didn't want to be rude. Her stepmother was stupid to think that she would ever be happy with a man like Londis. She would never love him. The king was a vampire, but Ida wouldn't allow her to even consider him, because that would actually make her happy. Maybe she could move past the fangs and the fact that he wanted her for her blood as well.

Her stepmother's words hurt a little, but she wasn't going to show her that. The king truly desired her, called her beautiful, and deep down Cindy realised she wanted to be his queen. Maybe it was unrealistic, but she had been dreaming about her true love ever since she was a little girl.

"I'm not marrying that obese man just so I can work on his farm like a slave. You can't just sell me off like livestock—you have no right. I had an invitation to the ball, so I had every right to be there, same as you, and I didn't need your permission. What happened with the king wasn't planned. It just happened," Cindy said, as calmly as she could.

Her stepmother started laughing, staring at Cindy like she was crazy. Cindy remembered the way she always put her down and made her feel worthless. Cindy cursed the day her stepmother entered her life and married her father. Everything would have been different if they'd never met. She loved her father dearly, but he was gone and she didn't have any other family.

"Yes darling, you're the true owner of the house and the estate, but as soon as you marry Londis everything will be legally transferred to me. And this wedding is going through, because once the King finds out that you're a hooker who works in the local brothel, he won't want anything to do with you," her stepmother said, with smug satisfaction in her tone.

Cindy dropped her jaw and then laughed a little. Her stepmother was crazy if she thought that her Caspian would believe such lies.

"I'm sorry stepmother, but your stupid plan won't work. I'm not a hooker, this accusation alone sounds completely ridiculous," Cindy stated, almost laughing. She was losing her confidence a little... The fairy hooker helped her that night to get to the ball, but Ida couldn't have known about it.

Her stepmother got up, went to the cabinet and took something out of the drawer and handed it to Cindy.

"Inside, there is a lease of the local brothel and your name is listed in one of the documents. Imagine what the whole town will think when they learn such a shocking revelation," Ida said. "You know yourself how fast news travels around here and once this rumour spreads to the king, he would never want to see or look at your face again. I have a witness who can confirm that he saw you the night of the ball inside the brothel, accepting a dress from another hooker. I want this house Cindy and I'm willing to do anything within my power to get it.

Your father had a weak mind, he had spoiled you rotten, and gave you everything you ever wanted. When I stepped in, it was already too late, Cinderella. I've never spoiled my girls; they're well behaved and they know what's acceptable and what's not. I've tried to keep you on the right path over the years, but it seems that I've failed."

Cindy started looking through the papers while her heart was racing away. She had no idea who had told her stepmother about Martha, or the fact that she went to the brothel last night. Her stomach dropped when she saw her name at the bottom of the document, along with the names of other girls from the brothel. She was convinced that the king wouldn't believe anything Ida said, but Cindy didn't tell him about Charles.

And once Ida spread this terrible rumour around, no one in the castle would accept that Caspian had chosen her.

She was so torn about him, but her feelings were real. Ida seemed to take Cindy's silence as encouragement to carry on.

"So this is what's going to happen. The king is arranging another ball. Apparently, the prince picked the woman he wants to marry and the king wants to celebrate in style. I've already spoken to Mr. Londis this morning and he's going to visit us tomorrow evening. This marriage is going forward, Cindy, whether you like it or not.   I will take ownership of your father's estate once you marry Londis. And unless you want the king to find out about the forest ranger or the fact that he ruined his reputation by getting involved with a hooker, then you will obey me. Mr. Londis is going to take you to the ball where you'll inform the king that you can't continue this affair, because you're already engaged to a respectable man. This will teach you a very valuable life lesson. If you would have listened to me from the very beginning, maybe this wouldn't have to happen. Besides, the king isn't for you, a man like him needs a real woman, someone who will stand by him and support him. You're immature, stupid and come from a toxic background. He will suffer to see you with someone else. Now, I want you to get on with your duties. You've already wasted too much of my time today."

Cindy's world was spinning out of control and the tiny voice in her head told her this wasn't really happening. She had no idea how, but her stepmother found a way to defeat her. Ida had a witness who could ruin Cindy's reputation, and Caspian was the King. He wouldn't want to get involved with someone like her, once he learned the truth.

Cindy was trembling, knowing that she was either going to lose her father's estate or Caspian. Ida had completely trapped her, and it looked like now Cindy had no other choice, but to marry that idiot Londis.

Red was wrong–nothing was going to end well for her. The king was a vampire, but she was ready to look past that. She wanted him, and her stepmother was wrong. She could see herself standing beside him.

"Yes, stepmother," she said in the end and left the room, feeling completely wiped and heartbroken that she'd lost this battle.

Chapter Eleven

Cindy cried when she went to feed the chickens later on. Her stepmother achieved what she wanted by faking the paperwork about her working in the brothel. Someone must have seen her with Martha that night, but the bar downstairs was empty. Almost everyone in town went to the ball. She didn't believe that one of Martha's girls would've betrayed her like that. A girl like Cindy never thought that she would be forced into marriage with a man who only wanted to use her as his farm worker and bed warmer. Especially now after her steamy night with the king.

The king had sent his guards to look for her, and tomorrow she would have to face him again, hand in hand with another man. She hadn't lied to him when he asked her if there was another man in her life. At the time, Cindy was convinced that she could still kick Londis up his backside. Now that seemed nearly impossible.

Her stepsisters laughed and mocked her while she worked. Cindy clenched her fists and carried on with her usual duties, ignoring their taunts as best as she could. Rage filled her veins, and tears of frustration built in her eyes, but she wouldn't let those wretched cows see her cry.

Everything was falling apart, and her dream of finding the love of her life was slowly fading away. Her stepmother hadn't said anything else to her since their confrontation, and Cindy finished all her housekeeping duties by midnight. She was exhausted when she went to bed, but couldn't sleep, yet again.

Londis—Cindy still had no idea what his first name was, and at that point she wasn't even bothered, nor did she care. In her new reality, she knew she was destined to stay unhappy for the rest of her life, but maybe it was fate's way of saying she didn't deserve anything better—her happiness died with her father. At some point, late in the night, she managed to drift off to sleep, dreaming about her wedding with the vampire king.

The next day, she considered running away from Ida and her stepsisters, but she knew that she had nothing but the clothes on her back. Everything that her father had left her— money, jewellery and some old antiques—was under Ida's careful watch and she highly doubted she could get away with taking back what was rightly hers with her stepmother guarding it like a hawk. Cindy knew her stepmother was a conniving woman—a liar—and she'd do anything to further her status in the kingdom.

In the evening, when Cindy saw Londis's carriage outside, she went to her room. Susan showed up a few minutes later, barking at her, telling her to get ready. She even threatened to drop a bucket of cold water over her head if she didn't hurry up. Although Cindy wanted to punch her in face, she had no other choice but to take out her red ball gown and put it on. It was getting dark outside when she entered the living room and saw Londis with her stepmother. Nausea rolled through her stomach, although she told herself that she couldn't act out of character in front of them; however, it would serve them right if she did indeed vomit on their shoes.

Teresa and Susan were staring at her with open jealousy as she walked in wearing the red ball gown Martha had gifted her in order to impress Prince Eric. Even Ida was surprised to see that Cindy had made such an effort. Londis kept staring at her boobs, nearly drooling. Tonight he looked as equally unappealing as when she saw him the first time. The thought of him touching her made her sick.

"Oh, there she is, Mr. Londis, our Cindy," her stepmother announced, giving her a stern look. "You can ride with your future husband in his carriage."

Cindy nodded. In a way she was glad that she didn't have to ride with her stepmother and stepsisters. She didn't want to listen to their ridicule or her stepmother's threats of blackmail. Teresa and Susan must have forgotten that Cindy looked much more beautiful than them, because now they were giggling to themselves, most likely happy that Cindy was so miserable.

"You look very delightful, but such an intense colour doesn't suit you at all. And it clashes with my suit," Londis commented, and Cindy sighed, ready to punch him as well. The king had complimented her dress multiple times, and he thought she was the most beautiful woman that he'd ever laid his eyes on. Obviously Londis had no clue about fashion, but either way Cindy didn't care about his opinion.

"I'm not changing, if that's what you're hinting at," she snapped at him when she stepped into the carriage.

"You should be more obedient. I expect that from my wife. We won't be going to any balls or parties when we're married," Londis said, spreading his legs in order to climb into his carriage. Cindy thought he was a fool if he thought for even a second that he could keep her locked up at his farm. She was a human being, and even if she married him, she would do what she pleased. "And you're going to serve my bed whenever I feel like it. It's a wife's duty to be obedient and spread her legs when her husband needs to feel satisfied."

Cindy's jaw dropped, and she instantly felt sick. She couldn't believe that Londis dared say something so disgusting to her. It looked like she wasn't only going to be his farm worker, but a sex slave as well. She was shaking with anger and didn't say another word to him the entire time they were riding together. However, Londis was yapping all the way to the palace about his farm, his animals and about how he imagined his new life with Cindy would be. By the time they arrived at the castle Cindy was ready to strangle him. Her stomach was rumbling, and on top of that, Londis had really bad breath. She had no idea how she was going to get through this horrible confrontation with the king.

Susan mentioned that when she was in town today, everyone was talking about her lace knickers. The king was still looking for her, and Cindy wasn't even embarrassed anymore that she'd spent a night with him.

She felt that her dress was stuck to her back when she walked inside the castle next to Londis. Every part of her body was aware that the king was nearby, but she wanted to avoid seeing him, knowing that it would break her heart.

Ida was walking behind her, looking proud and holding her head high. For the first time since her father passed away she realised that she hated her stepmother with a vengeance. Telling the king that she had to marry someone else was going to hurt Cindy in the worst possible way.

She had no doubt that Caspian would be devastated, and most likely furious that Cindy had lied to him.

Her stepmother and stepsisters were greeting other people in town. Cindy spotted Red in the distance, and she was surprised to see her with Charles again. The usual sparks that Cindy felt in the past when she saw him were missing; she just didn't care for the forest ranger anymore like she used to. She wanted to run away again, just so she could avoid being humiliated in front of the man she desired.

"I don't like these kinds of parties to be honest, but your stepmother insisted that I accompany you here tonight. I hope that we don't have to stay for too long. You shouldn't be staring at other men, you're going to be my wife soon enough," Londis said, as they both entered the ballroom. Cindy knew that Caspian had organised the second ball hoping that she would show up. It was torture for her to be there, standing on pins and needles waiting for him to approach her. Her stepsisters had already disappeared somewhere, and Cindy was glad that she didn't have to listen to their insults any longer.

"Cindy go and fetch Mr. Londis a drink," Ida asked, suddenly appearing next to her.

"Yes, stepmother," Cindy replied, thinking that she still had time to disappear. Her stepmother could let the king know that she was engaged without her being there, but Cindy wasn't a coward. Her father brought her up well and she was always ready to face her fears. The darkness still paralysed her, but she tried to overcome it and had done so after the first ball.

Cindy told herself that it was time to stop her pity party. She was strong and there was a way out of this marriage, she just had to figure it out. Then, a split second later, heat scorched down to her core. She knew the king had found her in the crowd, because Cindy instantly sensed him. Parts of her body tingled and sparks flew. No other man had ever made her feel like she was completely losing her mind, and she wanted to press her tingling body close to his. Vampire or not, he turned her sex into a pulsing bomb. He stood close, too close.

"Don't be afraid, my Cindy. I haven't been able to stop thinking about you since we made love. That's why I threw this ball tonight, because I knew you would come back to me," whispered the enigmatic voice behind her, sending cold shivers down her spine. She needed to close her eyes in order to calm down. All of this was happening too fast; she didn't even have time to think about what she was going to tell him."

"Please leave me alone, you don't want me. I'm not good for you. This will end badly for both of us," she said, not even knowing what was coming out of her mouth.

There was no way that she could turn around and look directly into his eyes. Maybe if she ignored him for a little while, he would leave her alone. His masculine scent was driving her crazy, and all she could think about was touching him again.

He placed his cold hand on her shoulder and her insides began melting away. She gasped for air, remembering every word and every moan that had escaped through her mouth the night that she spent with him.

"Leave? I'm not going anywhere. We must talk right away. I owe you an explanation. You ran away so quickly and I was losing hope thinking that I'd never see you again when my guards came back empty handed," he continued saying those soft words to her, making her forget where she was. Heat was turning her blood into lava. This wasn't really happening, her mind was in disarray. Pressure underneath her eyes was mounting.

"Cindy, there you are. I was just looking for you," said another voice that instantly brought Cindy back to reality. Her heart practically stopped when she realised that her stepmother stood next to the king, and she had dragged Londis along with her. Cindy's blood rushed to her ears and anger swamped through her body like a tornado. It was clear that Ida had been planning this from the moment she learned that Cindy had spent a night with the king. She was intentionally going to make Cindy look like a complete fool.

She knew that the king would eventually show up, and no doubt planned to interrupt her at just the right moment so she could hurt her further. She might as well have stuck a knife in her back and twisted it a couple of times.

"Your fiancé was just telling me how much he likes the castle," Ida said, smiling widely, but Cindy knew that it was a fake smile. She pretended that she didn't even notice the king in the first place and then methodically moved her gaze toward him. Cindy couldn't breathe, couldn't move. All her strength had left her body and she kept wishing for Martha to appear, so she could take her as far away from this place as possible. "I'm sorry, I don't believe we have been introduced. I'm Ida, Cindy's stepmother, and this is her future husband, Mr. Londis."

The vampire king looked at Cindy, then glanced at Ida, finally moving his gaze toward Londis. The awkward silence moved between them for a very long time and Cindy was ready to throw herself at her stepmother and throttle her. She finally looked up at the king, whose expression was stone cold, unreadable, and her heart sank even further.

"I'm King Caspian, pleased to meet you," he finally said. "A future husband? How can this be? I thought you were single, Cindy?"

Her stepmother laughed and Londis's mouth hung open. The king shifted closer and suddenly his presence was unbearable. Cindy was fighting with herself not to run away from them. She was considering telling him everything up front, but she had to find a way to be alone with him again, and right now that was impossible.

"Oh, our Cindy is so naughty sometimes and keeps telling lies, my lord. Mr. Londis has been in the picture for a very long time and the wedding is all planned out," Ida added, finally stabbing Cindy one last time.

"Is this true, Cindy?" the king asked in an icy tone of voice. Cindy had no idea what to say. Her stepmother was there and she didn't want to make a scene in front of the other guests.

"Yes, I'm engaged to Mr. Londis and we're going to be married very soon. This was my father's last dying wish," she admitted, wanting to scream that she had no other choice, but it was too late. The king exhaled sharply, and a dark shadow passed over his face.

"Very well then, I wish you the best. It was nice to meet you all, but please excuse me because I have some other duties that I need to attend to," he said, with the same cold voice, then turned and walked away.

Cindy was devastated, but she had done what was right, lied to him and herself.

"Who was that man? Someone said a king? He didn't look like royalty," Londis stated. "And I don't like the way he stared at my future wife, like she was a piece of meat."

"Oh Mr. Londis, you're such a joker," Ida laughed and then pushed Cindy towards him. "Come on, you must take Cindy around, show her off to the others. You two are so adorable."

Cindy was looking around for the king, but he'd already vanished in the crowd. The pain in her chest was rising, spreading down deep into her bones. It was just one night, and she had to forget about him if she wanted to keep her reputation intact.

She let Londis touch her, he wrapped her hand around his elbow and they started moving around through the ballroom. Now and again Londis made an effort to talk to her, but mainly she felt like she had no voice. In a matter of weeks, she was going to be stuck in the middle of nowhere without any way of getting out.

The mere thought made her sick to her stomach, knowing that she was going have to spend the rest of her life trapped in a loveless marriage, until her dying breath.

Chapter Twelve

"Ladies and gentlemen, please, may I have your attention. King Caspian has an announcement to make," the loud voice of one of the king's advisors spread throughout the ballroom.

The snippets and whispers moved throughout the crowd, and even Cindy looked up, curious to find out why the king wanted to address his guests.

Ida had gotten what she wanted, and despite the entertainment Cindy was ready to go home. Londis kept pushing her in front, suddenly looking very interested in royal affairs, but Cindy no longer cared. Sadness enveloped her, spreading through her veins—mind, body and soul—she was crushed.

She finally noticed him, standing behind his advisor. Caspian was by his son and the girl Prince Eric had picked up at the ball. Cindy didn't know her name, and she was surprised to see that Eric was planning to marry someone so unattractive, considering what he was saying at the ball. Cindy looked at Caspian, and again felt scorching heat spreading throughout her entire body, licking and touching every crevice. She knew that no one in the ballroom could tell that he was a vampire. People were so clueless.

He didn't even look at her once. She knew that he could sense her standing in the crowd. She deserved to be ignored. After all, she had lied to him in a sense.

"Cindy, keep still; otherwise I won't be able to see a thing. My knees are hurting," Londis complained when she was trying to stand on her tiptoes to see everything in front.

She rolled her eyes, and folded her arms over her chest. Londis was short. He barely reached her shoulders. Cindy thought about her wedding day, suddenly realising that she would look ridiculous standing next to him at the altar. She chose not to stare at the king any longer, although her heart was beating fast, and only for him, but their romance ended the night she ran away from the castle. His energy was making her wet, so she closed her eyes, trying to calm down, breathing in and out. He was so close, and yet so far away.

Finally, the crowd in the ballroom settled and people stopped talking. Caspian nodded to his advisor and stepped forward.

"I'm very delighted to announce that my son has found the woman of his dreams. Rigga comes from respectable family and in several weeks I'm planning to throw Eric a wedding party. Of course, every resident of the Farrington Kingdom is invited. Due to this special occasion, I'm announcing a national holiday tomorrow," the king stated, smiling, and the crowd erupted, cheering for him. Warmth danced around Cindy's chest, but she had a feeling that this wasn't the big announcement that she was waiting for. Moments later Caspian continued. "His decision made me realise that I should move on with my life as well."

The king paused for a second, like he wasn't sure if he wanted to continue, and then he found Cindy in the crowd. The heat from his gaze made her toes curl, and her breathing became laboured. She wanted to shout at the top of her lungs that she didn't want Londis. They were staring at each other, forming yet another silent connection. Cindy felt that she could love this man, but it was impossible, right? It was too soon to develop any feelings for him and yet she couldn't have been wrong. She was in love with the vampire king.

"As many of you know, my wife died almost twenty years ago and for a very long time I couldn't accept that she was gone. I've never met anyone who could make me happy the way she did. Seeing Eric filled with joy made me realise that I need to remarry too, that it's time for me to start over with someone who will love me like Catherine did," the king continued with his speech and then more snippets and whispers rolled through the crowd.

Cindy's heart sank and her knees nearly gave out. His voice kept ringing in her ears, and it seemed that people around her were suddenly very excited that they were going to have a new queen. The king was ready to find a new wife and several hours ago she could have been the one standing next to him.

The rest of his words faded as the buzzing in her ears became unbearable. Cindy glanced at her stepmother who was suddenly standing next to her. She must have walked up to her earlier to make sure that Cindy wouldn't do anything stupid.

"He would have never chosen such a pathetic creature like you. Londis is suited to you, and he will keep you in line."

Ida looked satisfied with the way things turned out, kicking Cindy while she was down. The king was still talking, but Cindy couldn't listen to him any longer. She was standing, rooted to the spot until his voice finally faded away. Sometime later, the music started playing again and everyone entered the dance floor. She was nauseous, and couldn't breathe when Londis grabbed her and told her that she owed him a dance.

Her body didn't feel like it belonged to her—she was numb and broken. The world she lived in seemed too cruel. Londis was leading her to the dance floor, saying something to her, but she was hurting everywhere and didn't hear anything he said. It felt like she was floating away into a state of nothingness.

People were smiling, looking like they were enjoying themselves while the orchestra played.

No one cared that the king had broken her heart or the fact that he was a vampire—that's if they knew at all. Her mind was tangled with questions about his age; she wondered if he drank human blood. She was a mixture of emotions and none of them good. She knew the king had to move on, especially after learning she was engaged to that pig, Londis, but if he knew the truth? Then what? More questions riddled her mind as she faded in and out.

"I'm sorry, I need to go to the loo, please excuse me," she blurted out to Londis and then pulled away from him. He was shouting something after her, but she wasn't listening. Her mind was in despair, tears dripping down her cheeks as she ran away. Cindy had to get away from the suffocating atmosphere, from judgmental looks and her evil stepmother. She found the door in the back of the ballroom and began rushing through the long, dark corridors, not even knowing where she was going.

Part of her soul felt like it had been torn to pieces, but she kept on going, moving as far away from the scene as possible. Soon she didn't hear the music anymore. Her chest started to burn, so she stopped for a second to steady her laboured breathing.

She happened upon a marble staircase and decided to climb to the higher parts of the castle, hoping to be alone. With darkness looming over her, old insecurities about being stuck in the darkness flared up. She needed to get away from Caspian, be as far away from him as possible. She missed him, but that didn't matter anymore.

The king had done something to her, twisted her heart, and now she couldn't function the same as before. Her stepmother was cruel, and Cindy was so stupid to have trusted her in the beginning.

Eventually she couldn't keep going, her legs were aching and sweat was running down her face. She sat down on the top of the stairs and cried. In the past, she had always remained strong and positive, but hearing Caspian talk about remarrying broke her from the inside out. She didn't know him, yes she slept with him, and that didn't give her the right to claim him as hers, but they formed an incredible connection that could easily turn into love.

She didn't want him to marry someone else, and her heart was crushing into tiny pieces at the thought of seeing him with another woman.

"Cindy? What's wrong? What are you doing here all alone along, spilling your precious tears?"

The voice startled her, and when she lifted her eyes she thought she was hallucinating. Caspian was supposed to be at the ball, so what was he doing in here with her? She swallowed hard and prickling heat scorched her skin as he stood in front of her. Every small hair on her body stood on end. She would recognise his scent anywhere; she knew that he was real.

He was beside her before she could even take another breath. In a matter of seconds, she had forgotten about her stepmother and Londis. Nothing else mattered when she was staring in the eyes of King Caspian, her vampire king.

"Nothing, it's nothing, I'm sorry," she mumbled, knowing that she couldn't really tell him what was wrong. If he knew that she was being forced into marriage, then he'd be furious. She couldn't risk the king learning of Charles or the fact that Ida had forged papers saying she was a hooker. His reputation would be ruined because of her, even if he knew she was a virgin when they met.

"You must tell me what's on your mind. I couldn't bear seeing you with that man, so I walked away. Why didn't you say anything sooner?" he asked, touching her, and warming her blood instantly.

"I was ashamed," she admitted.

"No, that isn't it. Tell me why you're really crying. What's going on, Cinderella?" he kept questioning her, but she couldn't concentrate when his cold fingers were touching her and burning her skin. She finally met his eyes and her thumping heart echoed inside her head.

"Because you announced that you were keen to take on a new wife," she whispered, and dropped her eyes, feeling embarrassed. "I can't bear it knowing that you will be with another woman."

He growled and before she could comprehend what was going to happen, he grabbed her face and kissed her hard. Cindy moaned into his mouth, losing herself completely to the only man that she could truly love.

***

The king was angry, furious with himself when he kissed her. He lost control when he saw her crying on the stairs. He needed to get away from the crowd, and finally be alone after he learned that she'd betrayed him. The craving for Cindy's blood was driving him insane. He pressed his mouth to her soft features, devoured her lips until she was gasping for breath.

It was so good to touch her again, and his cock was hard as a rock. She was spread over the marble staircase, moaning and whimpering. He'd been stunned, seeing her right outside his chamber, but it was a pleasant surprise. And after what happened at the ball he wasn't planning to let her go again.

"I'm going to fuck you hard right now, so you'll know who you truly belong to," he rasped in her ear and then ripped the top of her dress. Cindy's eyes were shut, but she moaned loudly, submitting herself fully to him. He was furious to learn that she belonged to another man, and yet satisfied that he took her virginity.

He stuck his face in her naked breasts and began to suck her hard nipples one by one, taking his time with each of them —they were just as glorious as he remembered. He couldn't get enough of her. Then he heard her, she was begging him to take her, to be inside her.

"I'm the one who makes the rules here, Cindy, not you. You need to remember that," he said, already moving his hand underneath her beautiful dress. This wasn't the best place to have sex with her, but the king was done caring if any of his people could hear them. He needed to fuck Cindy again, right now.

He nibbled on her neck, ready to sink his fangs into her veins, but somehow he managed to restrain himself. She wore stockings underneath, and it angered him. She was supposed to look sexy for him, only for him, and now he wanted to claim her as his. Her skin was soft and he was already addicted to her sweet scent that reminded him of a rainy summer day. His vampire instinct took over the moment he thought about tasting her blood, but he couldn't bite her, at least not yet. Besides, she needed to consent to it first. He wouldn't have done it otherwise.

"Please, I want you, please," she begged when he pulled her lace underwear down, and then slapped her arse. Caspian was ready to fuck her hard until she couldn't take it anymore. The first time they made love he was trying to be careful and gentle, but now he was raging inside.

He lifted her up and pushed her against the wall. The dress was wide, long and getting in the way, so he lifted it up, ready to tear it apart.

"Bend down; otherwise you will never see this beautiful dress ever again. I want to see that naked arse of yours," he ordered and Cindy obeyed him instantly, gasping for breath. Caspian was impressed that Cindy listened. He slapped her arse again and she cried out. His own power and being in control was turning him on, but he was done taking it easy on her. He pulled his pants down, releasing his erection and then kissed her again, biting her bottom lip hard, but not enough to pierce the skin.

She whimpered under him and he loved that she was so responsive, yet inexperienced. That big idiot she was going to marry couldn't compete with him. Cindy belonged to him.

"Oh yes, it's a wonderful view. Say that you belong to me, Cinderella," he ordered once again and then slapped her arse harder than before. She cried out and then he plunged his cock inside her.

"This feels so good, so good," she mumbled, pulling him back to reality. Cindy's sex felt like silk, moist and perfect and he knew that he was going to come at any moment if he didn't slow down.

Deep down, he couldn't, because he was furious that she had lied to him. When he found her, he was certain that she was upset because he announced that he was going to remarry.

Londis—that was the name of the loser who was apparently her fiancé. He couldn't imagine that a man like him could possibly take care of her. The whole story sounded unbelievable.

He grabbed her hips and kept moving until his head started spinning. The thirst for her blood was at the back of his throat, and he could already imagine how unbelievable she'd taste.

She looked so sexy when he was fucking her from behind, and he kept pounding into her, first nice and slow, then faster until she couldn't take it anymore. Her voice echoed in the entire corridor, probably letting everyone around him know what was going on out there. Caspian was the king and his entire staff could go to hell.

"Have you had enough, my dear, or do you want more?" he asked, knowing that the burning in the pit of his stomach was getting out of control. He was on the verge of coming while she moaned.

"Please, I can't take this, I need you," she pleaded, and then they both climaxed. The king's cock felt raw as he filled her with his semen, finally falling on top of her back.

For a long moment both of them tried to catch their breath, while Cindy's heartbeat was beating out of control. The King was still inside her and he knew couldn't possibly want any woman other than Cindy, but he was slowly beginning to realise that she already belonged to another man, and that was a hard pill to swallow.

It was either going to be the end of the beginning of something very special for him, or...

Only time would tell if he would have her again.

Chapter Thirteen

Cindy's body was feverish, and her heart was pounding rapidly in her chest. For a long moment, she had no idea where she was and how she ended up outside the king's chamber. She remembered running, being very upset at the ball and the next thing she knew, she was encased in the king's arms.

She heard Caspian's laboured breathing, and she was too afraid to move in case this was only happening in her head. Sadness filled her gut because she started to realise that she'd made a terrible mistake—the king could never be hers if she was forced to marry Londis. She wasn't being fair. However, their chemistry was real and none of it felt like a mistake—it was all so confusing.

On the contrary, Cindy was in love with King Caspian and that scared the crap out of her. The problem was that he was still a vampire, an immortal creature who fed on human blood and probably seduced other women. But Cindy wasn't worried; she didn't care that he could drain her life away. Their sex was addictive and she couldn't imagine functioning without him. She never felt anything like that towards any other man before.

"That was wonderful," she said, trying to reason with herself. Her stepmother and stepsisters were downstairs, and they were probably looking for her everywhere. Either way, the reality of the situation made her realise that there had to be another way. She had been taking orders from her stepmother for too long now and she wasn't a coward.

Ida and the deal that she made with Londis could go to hell. It was her life, and she was planning to live it her way.

Besides, her stepmother had no idea what she was talking about. Cindy could easily adapt to life in the castle. Her father was a man from the working class, and he told her to always be proud of who she was – he made his fortune the hard way. The king needed to marry someone who could rule his kingdom with him, and Cindy was willing to stand beside him as his wife and queen. She was well mannered, and she could learn necessary things, watch others in order to support him. It was an easy fix.

Time was moving slowly and then she felt him planting small kisses over her naked back. She wanted to enjoy this precious moment together for a bit longer. They were both exposed and anyone could have walked in on them. Cindy's heart pounded with love for the king. She just couldn't explain how she had fallen for him after only one night. She didn't want to go back to the ball and face Londis or her stepmother again.

Caspian finally pulled away from her and brought her into his arms. She felt his heart beating in his chest, and she was surprised. Her father had told her that vampires were dead. Maybe she had been wrong about the king all along.

"We have something special going on here," he said, and she instantly wanted to agree but had to keep her mouth shut. "I've announced that I need to get married, but there isn't anyone else that I want—it's only you. It's always been you."

"I have to marry Londis. At the time, when we met, it seemed I could get away from that stupid arrangement, but now I can't," she said, avoiding his eyes. She just couldn't look at him and pretend that she didn't love him.

"You never have to do anything that you don't want to do," the king snapped and Cindy thought that he was still angry over what happened earlier. She tried to put herself in his shoes, but couldn't.

She now believed in magic. Martha was a changeling and she changed beggars into a beautiful horses. Cindy thought about her again, wondering if she could help her in any way, but now it was a bit too late for that.

"Come on, put your dress back on. We have a lot to talk about and very little time. That evening, the night we met, I prepared a speech and then you ran away." He kissed her lips. She felt his fangs with her tongue, but kept calm. If he wanted to bite her, he would have done it already.

They both put their clothes on quickly, but Cindy hesitated going to Caspian's chamber. She needed to keep her spirits up, and her head was still high on lust from their steamy encounter.

In the end, she accepted his cold hand. Maybe her time was running out, and she was bringing too much attention to herself being away from Londis. Her stepmother was already watching her like a hawk, and Cindy didn't want to give her a reason to follow her everywhere.

"I'm not afraid of you, and I don't even know why," she said, reminding herself that her father always warned her not to trust strangers, especially those that were blessed with magic. He used to travel a lot, mainly between kingdoms, so he met many magical creatures on the road.

Cindy's heart was still pounding away when they climbed towards the king's private chambers. Her skin was burning up and she was still turned on. The king looked so handsome, and she wanted him to fuck her again. She wasn't even embarrassed about her own thoughts, thinking that maybe this was the last time that they were going to see each other.

"I could drain all of your blood and you would die. I could also twist your neck, so you should be a little afraid of me," he chuckled and brought her closer. "Especially after what happened downstairs."

"I know, but for some reason I can't think about fear when I'm around you. My stepmother is most likely looking for me already. I really need to go," she said, with a heavy heart. She didn't want to leave him and knew that if she dragged it out, it would be much harder to disappear. Caspian didn't look happy when he opened the door to his chamber and she walked inside anyway. She remembered every small detail of their night together. She wasn't even supposed to see him again. Now she was trapped.

"Do you really think that I will let you go after what just happened on the stairs?" he asked. "You aren't going anywhere.

I want you to sit down and let me explain everything. After that you can tell me why you're in such a rush."

Cindy liked the fact that the king was so assertive and took control.

"Tell me, how is it to be a vampire and live amongst humans?" she asked, but then felt a little silly. This conversation wasn't going anywhere. She was only making it more difficult for herself. She needed to find a way to screw up Ida's plans.

Caspian smiled, gesturing for her to make herself comfortable on the sofa. She noticed that she could see his fangs when he smiled, and wondered how it would have felt if he had bitten her neck.

"Be careful what you wish for. I can see in your eyes that you silently desire to be bitten," he growled and then grabbed her face. For a brief moment he stared into her blue eyes and Cindy felt like he saw how much effort it was taking her to keep her hands away from him. Then he kissed her again anyway, slipping his tongue into her mouth and her knees turned to jelly.

The tiny voice in her head kept reminding her that this what true love felt like. Her heart beat for this man—this creature—and all the new emotions were making her lose her mind. She knew that she would never feel anything like this with Londis. Not in a million years.

"How come other people don't know that you're a vampire? What about your son?" she asked, trying to pull herself together. "I thought that vampires couldn't reproduce."

"I can glamour people and make them believe that I'm just like them. And you are right. Vampires aren't supposed to father children, but several months after we met, my wife announced that she was pregnant. She was loyal to me and couldn't have slept with anyone else. I felt blessed, although it was a shock," Caspian explained, and Cindy knew that he most likely still grieved for his dead queen. He must have truly loved her.

"And no one knows? What about drinking human blood?" she pressed on, feeling a little excited about this part of the story. She wanted to know if Caspian preferred to drink from men or women.

"I have certain abilities. I can change appearance, and if I meet someone I can take over their appearance. This way it's easier for me to leave the castle. Besides, I only need to drink from humans once in a while." Caspian dragged his hand through his hair, exhaling sharply. Cindy thought that he was frustrated, and he still wanted her. She knew if she let him kiss her again she wouldn't be able to control herself the second time. They were here to talk and that was all.

"And there are other vampires in the kingdom? I mean, how did you become one?" she asked, sounding curious.

"Others exist, but they're hiding mostly underground or they're scattered around the country. We don't tend to keep together. It's easier to hunt alone," the king explained and Cindy wasn't sure what to think. Someone must have turned him into a vampire. She knew that much and maybe he just wasn't ready to talk about it yet. "My maker was old and was just about to die. He used my blood to gain strength and power. I was forty-five in human years when I become the bloodsucking monster I am now."

Cindy got up and sat next to him. She wanted to be close. Her body was betraying her, wanting and needing to experience his crazy lovemaking all over again. There was only so much control that she had in herself, but the voice of reason kept reminding her that even if she accepted the fact that he was a vampire, she still had to marry Londis unless by some miracle or magic, she could find a way out.

"So how long have you been forty-five?" she asked, and her voice vibrated a little. Caspian wanted her, but she would age eventually and die, while he would live forever. She was smart enough to realise that she wouldn't want him to see her old and wrinkled.

"I'm still only a young vampire and have been in this world stuck in this forty-five-year-old body for about twenty years. My first wife knew the truth and we were both concerned about our future. We talked about the issue of ageing a lot, and then she gave birth to Eric and was gone from this world," Caspian said. "I'm a creature of darkness and that comes with certain advantages. My abilities are very useful, Cindy, but right now I can't talk about it. You're distracting me, sitting here, and looking so innocent. I want to fuck you again."

Cindy swallowed hard and crossed her legs, aware that her sex was throbbing again. A moment later, he was on his knees, touching her feverish body. A loud moan escaped her. Luscious heat rose as he angled the kiss, pulling her harder towards him. They just had angry, intense sex and yet Cindy wanted more.

She was ready to forget about the ball and her stepmother and just stay with the king forever.

"No, no, we can't. I'm engaged to someone else. This isn't right," she said, trying to push him away, but he was already kissing her breasts and neck, and his lips felt so good. Her nipples were hard, ready to be touched as the desire filled the pit of her stomach. She was drenched with desire for him, her body was pumped with adrenaline, and then the king pulled away.

Frustration enveloped his features. He stood up and went back to the other side of the room.

"That man is not for you. We both know it, so how long are you planning to deny it?" he asked.

Cindy looked down at her hands, trying to find a way to explain to him that her stepmother had trapped her, but she felt too stupid to mention Charles. She was too naive trusting Charles in the first place, but thought to herself that the king needed to know what was going on.

She opened her mouth to tell him what Ida had done, but then felt magical energy hoovering over her body. She felt like she had something in her throat, and she wasn't even in control of her own voice – it was physically impossible to tell him. Someone had spelled her to keep her from telling the truth, but who?

"I'm not denying it, but you're a vampire, and you're lying to your people."

Cindy had no idea what was happening to her. It was like something magical manipulated her to turn his wild nature against him. She wanted to scream that Ida was blackmailing her, but her throat felt raw and painful. Caspian narrowed his eyes, and clenched his fists. He seemed angry, and Cindy was cursed. She couldn't physically tell him the truth.

"We're on fire when we're together, Cindy, and I don't want to share you with anyone else. You must tell that idiot that you aren't going to marry him. This is absurd. We're made for each other," the king said, sounding angry. He stood up and started pacing around the room.

Cindy looked at him with desperation, and she began to realise that something was very wrong, someone was trying to take control over her. She wanted to cry, but that wouldn't change a thing.

"I'm sorry, my lord, but this isn't possible. I have given my word," her own voice answered for her, like it had been programmed to do so. Her skin prickled with magic like during the time when Martha was turning beggars into horses. Her heart felt like it was being pierced by a million tiny blades.

She didn't look at him when she went to the door. Some wanted her to keep her mouth shut, and Cindy knew then that Ida had something to do with it. The king didn't stop her and that hurt like hell. Ten seconds later, she was running back to the ballroom, torn and frustrated. She heard a loud roar, and a bang. Caspian must have hit something out of rage, knowing that he had lost her again.

Eventually, she found the bathroom and cried until there were no more tears left in her. She knew that once she married Londis she could never see Caspian again.

She just couldn't experience the same pain all over again. The ball was still going when she returned. She noticed that her stepsisters were talking with two good-looking men by the punch table. Even Prince Eric was on the dance floor, leading his future wife to the rhythm of the music.

"You have no idea who you're dealing with, my Cindy. I have certain abilities that no one knows about, and you cannot disobey me. My magic will prevent you from telling the king the truth. The wedding is still going ahead as planned, and there's nothing you can do about it," Cindy heard Ida's voice behind her.

She turned around, but her stepmother was already walking away. Cindy tried to calm herself down, but she felt like she was drowning in a river of sadness. That was it, she had lost another battle.

Ten minutes later Londis found her, asking her where the hell she had been. Apparently, he had been looking for her everywhere. Cindy saw the king returning several minutes after her. He glanced at her briefly, but his eyes were empty, his usual spark was missing, and Cindy thought that this time she must have lost him for good.

Chapter Fourteen

"My lord, the ladies are here."

King Caspian lifted his head and realised that Jamie, his most devoted advisor, was talking to him. His thoughts were racing. Vampires couldn't get ill, but Caspian felt like he was under the weather.

"What are you talking about, Jamie?" he asked, more harshly than he intended. Lately he had been very hostile towards everyone and he offended a few people unintentionally. Deep down, he knew that Cindy had broken his heart. It was like he was reliving the moment when his beautiful wife had passed away and his world collapsed.

"The ladies that you asked for, my lord. They are all waiting for you in the main hall," Jamie repeated, staring at Caspian with concern.

Moments later, he remembered that a few days ago he had asked Jamie to find suitable women that he could meet beforehand. He made this hasty decision straight after he found out that his Cindy was marrying another man. He still couldn't comprehend why he didn't stop her. He spent only a few hours with her, and the sex was unbelievable, and yet he let her leave a second time. He just wasn't ready to accept that he'd lost her forever.

He frowned wondering what the hell was wrong with him. He didn't want to speak to other women, but it was too late to back away and he hated disappointing humans.

"Right, I should be there in a minute. Just give them some champagne," Caspian said, dragging his hand through his hair. Even his body felt tired and drained. This never happened to him before. It was like he was rotting from the inside out, losing part of his human soul.

Caspian was an impulsive man and he hated when things didn't go his way. He knew that this was one of the weak traits of his character. He didn't really think about the consequences of announcing that he was planning to remarry. Cindy made him furious and he just thought that he would punish her, knowing she was at the ball and would have heard his speech.

He took her virginity during the first ball. And after she left, he thought that he could spend the rest of his life with her.

Then he found her on the stairs, crying her eyes out and he instantly regretted that he publicly humiliated her.

His Cinderella was pure and innocent.

Jamie nodded, bowed and then left the king alone. Caspian wasn't ready to greet a bunch of women who showed up to meet him. No matter how many more Jamie invited over, he only wanted one woman—Cinderella.

Five minutes later, he was up on his feet walking through the long corridor. He approached the door, counting at least ten ladies inside. He opened the door and stepped inside, releasing his glamour. All the ladies stopped talking all of a sudden and stared at him looking excited. The king admitted that they were all very beautiful, and Jamie had done well, because they were mostly around his age. Still, Caspian just didn't care for any of them.

"I'm afraid there has been a mistake, my dear ladies, the king is not feeling well today and had to retire to his chamber. Please follow Jamie back towards the castle gate," he stated, using his vampire abilities to make them believe that he wasn't the king.

Several seconds later, the women started walking through the door, looking disappointed and a little confused. Jamie was already directing them towards the lower parts of the castle. The king went back to his chamber feeling conflicted. He didn't really sleep that much these days. He was hungry too, but he wasn't ready to leave the castle tonight. Cindy had woken him from a dream. It seemed like Caspian had been stuck in his own routine for twenty years, just wading through life.

He thought about his dead wife, trying to remember their brief time together. The craving for human blood wasn't going away and a few hours later he decided that he needed to satisfy his hunger.

Caspian was still a young vampire, but he could sense when someone was lying to him and there was something that Cindy wasn't telling him. Her stepmother had some kind of control over her. Caspian was ready to fight for her, but needed to get to the bottom of the truth.

He quickly changed into some old clothes and then transformed his appearance into a hunter that he once met in the forest. It was the perfect opportunity for Caspian to sneak out of the castle that evening. Eric was traveling to another kingdom to meet Rigga's parents. The preparations for the wedding were well under way, and Caspian needed to take his mind off Cindy. The anger inside him was transparent and raw. He wasn't ready to give up on her, but he had no idea what to do. He thought that once he satisfied his hunger, he would be able to think more rationally.

Half an hour later he was outside the castle gates. The air was cool and the temperature was a bit on the low side tonight. The king inhaled oxygen into his lungs, smelling the faint scent of human blood. He never killed his victims. He drank their blood and then he made them forget about it. This way no one ever suspected anything.

His senses were much sharper tonight and he left the castle grounds soon enough, entering the forest. He heard humans around, mostly peasants and a few hookers that were fooling around in the bushes.

Caspian avoided the hookers until he reached the outskirts of town. He spotted a young man who was tending to his horses in the stables, humming a well-known ballad to himself. The king's throat was burning and he decided not to wander off anywhere else.

Using his inhuman speed, he caught the man by his throat and sank his fangs right into the crook of his neck. His blood was delicious, and he instantly felt better as the precious liquid began flowing down his throat. The man was most likely in his mid-twenties, and the king glamoured him right away, so he wouldn't feel any pain.

His vision and hearing became hypersensitive and was able to sense when the man's pulse began to slow down, an indication that Caspian needed to stop draining him. Caspian was a vampire, but he still considered himself a good man. Before he was turned into a bloodsucking monster, he worked as a carpenter in another kingdom in order to support his parents.

As soon as he laid the man on the ground, he heard a woman's scream. He quickly covered the two puncture wounds with his blood and ran into the forest. The peasant boy would be unconscious for some time, but once he woke up, he wouldn't remember a thing. The king's strength came back from the blood, and it didn't take him long to locate the woman in need.

"Just try and touch me, you dirty pig, and I will rip off your bollocks with my teeth," the king heard the woman snarl.

Behind the trees he saw that she was surrounded by at least three dirty-looking men. Caspian assessed that they were the local thieves that one of his advisors had told him about several weeks ago. They had been terrorising the people from around town for quite some time now, and someone needed to teach them a lesson.

The woman had a small knife in her hands, she wore a red silky cloak with a hood covering her head and the king had to admit that she was very beautiful. Even if she knew how to defend herself, she wouldn't stand a chance. All three thieves were stronger and most likely much quicker than her.

They all laughed at her, approaching her from each side. A dark-haired thief with multiple scars on his face tried to grab her, but she cut his palm. Caspian was impressed and thought that she handled herself well. At the same time, the other crept up on her from behind and quickly wrapped his elbow around her throat. The third one didn't waste any time. He pulled off her red cloak, grabbing her breasts, while she tried to untangle herself, screaming obscenities and threatening to kill him.

"You need to go down on your knees, my love, and suck my dick. It's been a long time. Besides, I like girls with a dirty mouth," the one with the cut said, and then licked her face. The thief behind her laughed out loud. The girl was swearing, trying to kick the one who held her, but she wasn't strong enough to fight them all.

The king had seen enough. It was time for him to reveal himself. He stepped out from behind the trees and whistled loudly. His frustration over what had happened with Cindy took a toll on his mood, and he was ready to hurt those scumbags.

"Gentlemen. I suggest you step away from this lady as soon as possible or you'll certainly regret it," he said loudly. The girl looked at him and Caspian noticed her incredible, honey-gold eyes.

The thieves backed away from the girl, startled by his appearance, and the two of them lifted their sharp knives, glancing at each other with apprehension.

"I don't need your help, stranger. Go away before they kill you," the girl snapped, and Caspian was surprised. She wasn't scared and still wanted to fight. Each of the thieves wanted to rape her. The king could smell their lust, and saw the thrill of excitement in their eyes.

"Listen to the girl, hunter, or feel the sharpness of my blade," the one with the cut face stated, spitting on the ground. His three companions laughed, and the girl looked around desperately, like she was considering running away. Caspian wiped his mouth, still tasting the peasant's blood on his tongue.

The thief with scars attacked first, launching himself and trying to stab the king in his gut. He wasn't fast enough. Using his inhuman speed, Caspian bit his collar bone. The thief went down, not even knowing what had happened, dropping his blade. He was instantly unconscious. At the same time, the girl kicked the thief that had his elbow around her neck right between his legs. He had no other choice but to release her, moaning in agony. In a matter of seconds, the girl vanished somewhere between the trees.

Caspian thought that she was fast, but he couldn't chase after her through the forest, because the other two thieves were on him now. He kicked one with his foot and then punched him, breaking his nose. The man struggled, his eyes rolled into the back of his head, and then he went down like the first one. He bit the smallest one with his sharp fangs, but didn't drink from him. Caspian sensed that his blood wasn't pure, so he left him lying on the ground. He needed to remember to send his guards out later to arrest the thieves. They weren't going to be waking up for the next few hours.

It was late and the moon finally appeared from behind the clouds, shining brightly. He was still a little concerned about the girl with the red cloak, so he set off to find her. The girl wasn't far, and with his vampire abilities he was already tracking her down. He sensed a few wolves around and suddenly the king was concerned about the girl's safety. He started moving through the bushes and circulating between the trees, until he heard the wolves howling in the distance.

Then, out of nowhere someone jumped on him, knocking him off his feet. It took him several moments to realise that he was being attacked by a petite, dark-haired girl. He recognised her scent from earlier on and now she held a small knife pressed down to his throat.

He was impressed; she was faster than he expected.

"Who sent you, scum? I know that you've been following me around for hours now," she snarled at him, threatening to cut him. The king wanted to laugh, staring at her beautiful golden eyes and dark hair. She was a local and knew her way around the forest well, so he assumed she knew Cindy.

Caspian had wasted enough time. Tonight he was planning to find her. After what happened between them, he wasn't ready to just let her go and wouldn't accept that she was marrying someone else.

"I haven't been following you. I'm looking for someone and I was only trying to help you," he chuckled and the girl only narrowed her eyes at him with anger. Caspian thought that she wouldn't hesitate to kill him if needed.

"And do you think I'm just going to believe you," she snapped. "Who are you looking for?"

"Cindy, the blond girl with beautiful blue eyes. Do you know her?" he asked, hopeful. The girl studied him for a long while, and her expression softened a little. The king knew that he struck gold. It seemed that she knew his Cindy.

Eventually, she pulled her knife away and hid it in her boot.

"What do you want with her? The stupid girl is going to marry some farm man soon, believing it'll save her blasted reputation. If you ask me she's a fool," the girl said, shaking her head.

Caspian's emotions ran wild and he was ready to throttle the girl to make her tell him everything. Somehow he managed to restrain himself. The girl with the red cloak finally got off him and they both stood up. She had a sharp gaze and the king knew that he made a good decision to go for a hunt tonight.

"Tell me all about this marriage," he requested, straining his muscles. He knew that Cindy was lying to him.

"There's nothing to tell. That fool is marrying the fat pig. Besides, it's too late to stop her. She already left with her stepmother and that farmer for another Kingdom. I had a feeling that her stepmother was planning to marry her off in order to take over the estate. Her father had put some sort of clause in his will, his last dying wish or something. Cindy's been acting strangely, as if she has no other choice but to marry that man," the girl said. "Sorry, but you better forget about her. She's a lost cause."

Chapter Fifteen

Cindy was leaving Farrington Kingdom behind, and her beloved vampire king. She was stuck in the carriage with Londis, while her stepmother and stepsisters were riding in front. Her husband-to-be was snoring loudly next to her and she was trying really hard not to burst into tears. Ida had put a spell on her, knowing that she would try to tell Caspian the truth. Cindy should have gone to the King sooner, and maybe now she would be free.

It looked like her stepmother didn't waste any time. She announced that Cindy, Susan and Teresa were to accompany Londis back to his cottage. Then she proceeded to tell Cindy the wedding plans were well on their way too. Apparently, Londis liked the idea of a quick marriage and he wanted Cindy to start working on his farm as soon as possible.

They had already been on the road for a few hours and Cindy couldn't stand being with Londis any longer. Maybe Ida was sensing that Cindy could change her mind at any moment, so she wanted to rush things. Cindy had lived with her long enough to see through her evil plan. She'd told Cindy to pack as soon as they got home from the ball.

She tried to sleep for another two hours, but Londis was snoring so loudly that she eventually gave up. At some point, the carriage finally stopped and when Cindy looked out the window she saw an obscure cottage that stood on the edge of a field. Londis truly lived in the middle of nowhere. Cindy tried to find a silver lining, but there was none.

Behind the house was Londis's farm. She noticed he had pigs, goats and other animals. He had a lot of land and she knew that once she married him, she would be stuck there for the rest of her life.

"This place is such a dump, and I'm so glad that mommy decided to send Cindy here," Susan said, entering Londis's cottage.

"Cindy, take our luggage inside. The wedding will be in two days at the local church. Your fiancé has already made you an appointment with the local dressmaker," Ida said, smiling away like this was the best day of her life.

Cindy nodded and started dragging their heavy belongings inside the house. Her stepsisters were already laughing that she would be stuck with pigs all day long, telling her that this was where she belonged.

"Come on, my Cindy, I'll show you around," Londis said, appearing right in front of her. "You'll be working very hard around here and on the weekends I normally sell meat at the market." He didn't offer to help her carry the heavy luggage. It seemed that Cindy's new life was already well planned out. A sick feeling and general sense of dread and pressure was building in her chest. On top of that, she was expected to have sex with this man, and wanted to vomit even thinking about it.

He showed her around the farm once she made a cup of tea for her Ida and her stepsisters. Londis mentioned that the town was several miles away and that she needed to be careful after dark, because the wolves sometimes wander over, killing the sheep.

Londis's life was very basic. The cottage had running water, but when Cindy saw her married bedroom, she was horrified. Their bed was tiny and most of the space was filled with packages of meat. Cindy had no idea what to think, and went to the other room where she was supposed to sleep tonight.

She and Londis weren't married yet, so Ida decided that they should still have separate beds. Cindy was glad that she still had some time before she was expected to sleep with Londis.

When the sun set behind the horizon, she was lying in bed, thinking about her steamy encounter with the king. She had no idea how and when, but she had to find a way to see him one last time.

***

"I think it's very simple and it will make you look humble, Cinderella, exactly the way a girl like you should look during the wedding," Ida was saying while Cindy was standing on the stool wearing the ugliest wedding dress that she'd ever seen in her life. The dress was supposed to be white, but it was almost grey and it looked like the dressmaker had pulled it from the garbage bin. It was covered with yellow lace and she could barely breathe in it.

She couldn't help recalling Martha and how she'd dressed her in the most stunning dress for the ball. They had been running all day long, trying to sort everything out for the wedding. Her stepmother was really determined and she was haggling over every cent.

Cindy didn't know anyone in Gardland's Kingdom, and she had no idea who her stepmother invited to the wedding party tomorrow. She expected to see Londis's family, but everyone that Cindy knew was still in Farrington. She stood, staring at her ugly wedding dress, refusing to break in front of her stepmother. She didn't want to give Ida another cause for celebration over her small victory.

"Yes, stunning. I bet your fiancé will fall in love with you all over again," the obese dressmaker said, but Cindy thought she had a fake smile.

"Good. Cindy, take the dress off and let's pack it all up. We also need to run to the baker and make sure they're done with the cake," Ida added sweetly.

Cindy stepped down from the stool and went to the back to change into her normal clothes. The tiny voice in her head reminded her that she still had time, that no one would know if she ran away. She quickly shook her head, took the dress off and looked at herself in the mirror.

Her complexion was sullen, and for some reason she looked ill. She told herself that she had to fight for her dreams. She couldn't just give up.

"Cindy, hurry up, we haven't got all day. I want you to run over to the tavern and tell my daughters to meet us at the bakery." The squeaky voice of her stepmother interrupted her thoughts.

Cindy nodded and dressed quickly, considering all the pros and cons. She had no money on her, but she had to find a way to stop this stupid wedding. She left the dressmaker shop five minutes later and headed towards the north side of the town where her stepsisters were drinking in the tavern. They were most likely flirting with some locals, having the time of their lives, as usual.

Her breathing was laboured as she rushed through town. Cindy knew that this was her last chance to run away. She needed to get back to Farrington Kingdom somehow, to her home before Ida realised that she was gone. She knew where her stepmother kept a stash of money. Cindy could use it to get to the king. Maybe she could find a way to break Ida's spell and tell him everything. Either way she had to try something. She was done being a doormat.

She saw the local tavern from the distance and stopped by the butcher to catch her breath. Her plan was crazy, she realised that, but she was desperate enough to try anything at that point.

"Have you heard? The King of the Farrington Kingdom is looking for a wife," said a woman who just left the butcher's shop. Cindy froze, thinking that they couldn't have been talking about Caspian. He announced at the ball that he wanted to remarry, but he was only trying to punish her. Cindy didn't expect him to go through with it.

"Oh my, so have you heard if he found the right woman?" the other girl asked, giggling to herself.

"Don't know, but I heard that he lined up a few, and he's meeting others too. I'm shocked that he's not looking for someone with royal status, but then his own son picked some ugly duckling too," the older woman added, and they both giggled.

Cindy's head started spinning, but she should have known that the king wasn't going to wait for her.

"King Caspian is so damn good looking, and he deserves to be happy. At the same time, I think he shouldn't rush with such an important decision."

"Yes, his future wife should have class. His dead wife was loved by his people and she had a heart of gold," the younger one said.

The women left her, heading towards the square, still engaged in their conversation.

That was the last straw for Cindy. She needed to get away from there, from Londis and her stepmother. She was ready to scream at the top of her lungs that the king had chosen her, and she wanted him too. She glanced around in desperation, but she didn't know anyone in that stupid town and didn't want to bring any more attention to herself.

Before she could even think about what she was doing, she turned abruptly around and started running in the opposite direction. She was done taking orders from any member of her so-called "family" and needed to think about her future. Running away was the only option, and in a way she had a bit of an advantage. She knew that Ida would be pissed off that all of her preparations would be ruined, but Cindy didn't give a flying monkey anymore. This was her life and she was desperate enough to disappear right under Ida's nose.

By the time she reached the forest it had started raining. Cindy spent all day running after her stepmother and now it was getting dark. Her old fears were spiking her anxiety and she felt like she couldn't breathe. She hadn't thought about her fears when she made a decision to go back to Farrington. Large bricks of nausea filled her stomach, and she was slowly feeling paralysed, unable to walk through the darkness. This happened the night of the ball, but somehow she'd forced herself to keep going. So she kept walking, not knowing if she was even heading in the right direction.

At some point, she must have reached the road because she heard horses galloping behind her. She was wet, hungry and scared. The coachman must have taken pity on her because he stopped the horses and asked, "Where are you going, girl? Need a ride?"

Cindy no longer cared if it was safe to be picked up by some random stranger, but she couldn't bear being in the dark any longer. Blood was rushing to her ears, and she just knew that she would be torn apart by some wild animal if she didn't accept the coachman's offer.

"Farrington Kingdom," she mumbled, thinking about Martha and wondering if the hooker would be willing to help her again. The man had a long shaggy beard and kind eyes. Cindy knew better, she shouldn't really trust him, but at that point there was no way she could turn around and go back to her stepmother.

"Hop in, I'm going that way. There's a lady and a gentlemen in the carriage. Just sit with them and be quiet," he said, and Cindy couldn't believe her luck. Someone opened the door and she sat opposite a high class lady and a gentlemen who looked like he was sleeping. She tried to breathe in, to somehow pull herself together, because now she was away from the darkness. Still, her heart pounded in her chest like she was about to go into cardiac arrest. The carriage started moving and eventually she must have fallen asleep, exhausted.

The next thing she knew someone was shaking her slightly, saying, "We're in Farrington, girl. I'm heading home to my wife. You can't stay in the carriage. Do you have somewhere to go?" he asked her. It took her a moment to remember what had happened and where she was.

"Yes, yes. Thank you so much. I'll be on my way," she responded, stepping out onto the road. She recognised the building and saw the castle in the distance. Her heart warmed up a bit and her worries slipped away. Her king was there and she needed to see him, but not tonight. She had to get to her home first or find Martha. Either option sounded reasonable enough.

It was really late and Cindy knew that Ida wouldn't travel back in the middle of the night. Besides, Ida knew about her fear of the darkness and most likely assumed that Cinderella wouldn't have enough courage to go all the way back to Farrington. That should have bought her some time, and at least she was filled with new hope.

Now she was standing in her kingdom, the place where she was born, and had no idea what to do. Gripping fear paralysed her again, but she was convinced she'd just made the best decision of her life. She was done with her stepmother for good. The moon was shining brightly and Cindy swallowed hard, telling herself that she was home. She didn't have to be scared anymore, and she just had to conquer the fear dwelling inside of her.

If she really wanted to survive in this world and stop being weak, she needed to move. It was now or never. It was up to her to follow through with her crazy plan. No one could tell her what to do—it was her life and she had to fight for her happiness, even if it felt almost impossible.

Chapter Sixteen

Caspian was filled with optimism and new energy after returning to the castle late last night. He thought that his unexpected encounter in the forest with Red Riding Hood couldn't have come at a better time.

He accompanied Red back to her cottage and they talked about his beloved Cinderella. The king didn't want to ask too many questions, he wasn't ready to reveal his true identity to Red. The more Red talked about Cindy's arranged marriage, the more he was convinced that she was being used. He sensed that her stepmother didn't have her best interests at heart. She must have manipulated Cindy into the marriage with the old farmer. The king believed that she was trying to make some sort of business deal with her naive, sweet stepdaughter none the wiser. The funny thing was that Caspian remembered Cindy's father. Years ago, when his Catherine was still alive, he sold him a very well-made rug.

Red also took him to Cindy's house, the estate that used to belong to Cindy's father. The king had another problem. Red was convinced that Cindy was getting married tomorrow, and that only gave him a small window of time in which to act. He wasn't sure what to do.

The castle was immersed in silence while he was pacing in his chamber. Then he spoke to a few advisors, asked them to spread some rumours around the kingdom that he was going through with his search for a new wife. Caspian needed to track her down, but had a feeling that he was already too late. He clenched his fists, knowing that she couldn't marry that fool.

In a last resort he was ready to send his troops out in order to find her and bring her back to the castle.

That night he didn't sleep, as a vampire he didn't have to anyway. Sometimes he liked pretending that he was still a human, especially when Eric was growing up. At some point he must have drifted off, but his mind was still working overtime.

He was up again around six a.m., walking around the chamber, ready to jump back on his horse and travel to Gardland's Kingdom that morning in order to find her. His son was getting married in a couple of weeks, and after the king's announcement, Eric thought that Caspian was moving too fast. The king had been alone for over twenty years and Eric thought that his father was planning to steal his glory.

At seven a.m. his personal butler brought his breakfast in as usual. The king didn't need to eat, but people needed to believe that he was just like them.

"Is there anything else that you need, my lord?" Rudolf asked, staring at him like he knew the king was concerned about something.

Caspian dragged his hand through his hair, thinking about his answer when someone barged inside his chamber. It was Jeremy, one of the assistants who worked in the kitchen; he couldn't have been more than sixteen years old. His chest was rising and falling in rapid movements and it looked like he had been running all the way to king's chamber.

"My lord…my lord. Sorry for intrusion, but Dominic sent me to speak to you. It's early and I was afraid—"

"It's all right, just start from the beginning. What's going on?" Caspian asked, waving to the butler to leave them alone. The boy placed his hands on his thighs and took long pulls of air. People in the castle always respected him. They knew that he was fair and he looked after them well.

Jeremy nodded and king handed him a glass of water. The boy looked like he could do with a drink. After a few minutes he finally started making sense.

"There's a man in the courtyard with a lady. They're both demanding to speak to you, my lord. Constant doesn't want to let them in and keeps telling them that they should come back at more appropriate time, but they are refusing to leave," Jeremy explained and the king frowned. He wasn't expecting anyone and wasn't in the mood to resolve some kind of conflict between two peasants.

"Constant is competent enough to deal with them," Caspian snapped. He was wasting time this morning, and Cindy was somewhere out there, probably already getting ready for her wedding day.

"He has tried to reason with her, but that woman insists that you know something about this girl who's gone missing. She isn't prepared to speak to anyone but you, my lord," Jeremy explained.

"A girl's gone missing?" Caspian repeated.

"Yes, the woman insists that you know something about her."

Caspian shifted in his chair, then got up and headed to the door, forgetting about his breakfast.

"All right, let me speak to them," he muttered more to himself. He was heading towards the direction of the stables anyway and needed to see what this peasant woman wanted from him.

He didn't think that this issue had anything to do with Cindy, but it was a possibility. Her stepmother had found out that he spent a night with her. And he sent his advisors around the kingdom several days ago to find her, using the only other item of clothing that he had left—her lace knickers. Jeremy followed behind him.

Ten minutes later, Caspian walked through the main hall and new hope flickered through him. In the distance, he saw Cindy's stepmother and her future husband. They were arguing with Constant who looked like he was just about to lose his temper. A few other guards gathered around them too.

"What is the meaning of this?" Caspian asked, approaching the group. He remembered Cindy's stepmother from the ball, and he instantly took a dislike to her.

"My lord, my lord. Please allow us a few minutes with you. My stepdaughter, Cindy, has gone missing," the woman said, rushing to him. She looked upset, but the king wasn't sure if she was concerned for her safety or the fact that her carefully prepared plan was suddenly falling apart.

"Yes, it's our wedding day today and she vanished last night. We were in Gardland's Kingdom. I don't understand why, but Ida believes that this stupid girl might have come back to Farrington," the man named Londis said, shaking his head. None of this made any sense to Caspian. First of all, her stepmother mentioned that Cindy went missing, but their story made him believe that she simply decided to run away. Maybe she realised that she couldn't live without him, so she came back to Farrington. Either way, the wedding wasn't happening and he needed to find her.

"It's all right, Constant. Let's move to the conference chamber where we won't be disturbed," the king said, and then showed Ida and Londis the best place where they could talk.

It looked like Cindy wasn't going to listen to anyone and he liked that about her. She wasn't as weak as he thought. Caspian's expression remained neutral, but in his mind, he was already imagining having her in his arms again. Once they moved to the conference room, Ida started telling him that the whole wedding had been arranged—the venue, the musicians and church. Gardland's Kingdom was a few hours horse ride away.

"She must have been kidnapped or taken against her will. We were doing the last fittings for her dress and then I sent her away to tell my other daughters to meet us at the bakery, and she vanished," Ida said, and fresh tears spilled down her cheeks "We thought that maybe you, my lord, might have heard something. You were so fond of her at the ball."

"Yes, I must ask for your assistance, my lord, as a proud resident of Gardland's Kingdom. The wedding plans have been put on hold and I have so many relatives who are travelling from all parts of the country to celebrate with us. Cindy must be found soon," Londis said, and Caspian was angry, furious that this man was treating his precious Cindy like livestock. It seemed to him that no one asked Cindy if she truly wanted to marry this man.

"I'm afraid that Cindy hasn't come to see me if that's what you're asking, but I will send out a search party right away," he assured them. "But I have to ask—maybe Cindy was unhappy perhaps and she simply ran away to avoid being married. Of course it's not my intention to disrespect anyone here."

Ida paled and glanced at Londis who still had a stupid expression on his face. Caspian was playing a game with them, and he was glad that Ida and that fool came to see him. Now he could track Cindy down on his own terms.

"No, of course not, my lord. It was love at first sight between her and Mr. Londis. They were so happy together and now we're all concerned about her safety," Ida replied quickly, but the king sensed that she was lying to him. Cindy couldn't love that fool, Londis.

"Yes, she was looking forward to her new life on the farm," Londis said, stroking his fat jaw. "Her living situation in Farrington was a bit more comfortable, but that doesn't change the fact that we were perfectly matched."

Caspian didn't want to hear anymore. Ida must have made some sort of deal with Londis, and the king needed to get to the bottom of it. She married Cindy's father for a reason, and then he left her everything? None of it made any sense.

"Please leave this to me. We will find her," he said simply, indicating that was the end of the conversation. He walked to the door, and Ida continued to thank him, still crying and saying that she was really concerned about her stepdaughter's safety.

As soon as they were gone, he called Jeremy back into the room. "Follow them. I need to find out what their intentions are towards Cinderella. I have a feeling that she's being forced into marrying that foolish man."

Jeremy looked a little surprised, but quickly assured Caspian that he would find out as much as he could.

The king smiled to himself thinking that he had to pay someone a visit. It was time and he couldn't wait any longer. Either way she wasn't going to marry Londis, because her heart belonged to him.

***

Two hours later, after leaving the castle and wandering around the forest, the king located the old cottage hidden in the deepest parts of the woodland. Many years ago, he promised himself that he would never again seek the help of the old witch again, but current circumstances forced him to look for her once more.

She was the one person from his past he knew could help him. He was turned by a sadistic vampire who only used him to survive. He didn't tell Cindy the whole truth about his past. His maker nearly killed him when he was attempting to transform him into a vampire.

Caspian was dying when he escaped from the creature who drained his blood. He wandered around the forest for hours, before the old witch found him. She was skilled, and her magic was much more powerful than the magic of fairies. She nursed him back to health, and he owed her a favour. She never claimed it back, but told him that one day he would come seeking her help once again. Over the years, he'd forgotten about her, and she never sent for him even when he became a king.

Smoke rose out of the chimney and he sensed her inside. The old witch was much more powerful than him, but he never trusted her. He thought that she secretly took his blood when she attempted to heal him, that's why he never came back. Then a split second later, the door opened and he saw her standing in the shadow, leaning over a long stick.

"I thought you had forgotten about me, vampire king," the old woman said.

Caspian's past flashed right in front of him, and his craving for blood burned his throat. He sensed magic circulating around him; her energy was still vital. Nothing had changed after twenty years, but he noticed that she'd aged.

"I need your help old witch, and your magic," he said as he approached her. She was an old woman, with long grey hair and wrinkles marring most of her face. The king was surprised that she was still alive, although it seemed that her magic hadn't diminished with age. Caspian remembered those green eyes that were now staring straight through him.

"You're in love and you think that you're about to lose her. Don't worry, I can help you. There's always a price that people are willing to pay for love," she said, and then gestured for him to enter the cottage.

The king hesitated, but he knew that he had to sacrifice something for Cindy. He couldn't lose her like he had his first wife, Catherine. The cottage had a low ceiling and was supported by old wooden beams. There was a table and chairs, and a large pot was boiling in a fireplace filled with logs. The cottage smelled of sage, thyme and blood. The witch must have slaughtered an animal there earlier, because the king could smell it everywhere.

"You know where she is and who she truly loves?" he asked. The old witch smiled, humming an unknown song to herself, and stirred a strange substance inside her huge pot.

"Yes, I possess all the knowledge you seek," she replied after some time. "But you need to make a decision. Are you ready to give away your immortality in order to have her love?"

Caspian didn't want to spend the rest of his life utterly alone. And he couldn't lose her. The old witch could have asked for anything, and yet he didn't expect her to demand his immortality.

"I'm willing to do anything to save her," he finally said. He was ready, ready for anything to have a life with Cindy.

Chapter Seventeen

"Unbelievable, girl, that stepmother of yours is a real bitch," Martha shouted, placing her hands on her hips.

Cindy smiled weakly, chewing her nails as the reality of what she had done was making her a bit queasy. It had been twenty-four hours since she ran away and headed back to Farrington Kingdom and her own wedding was supposed to start in six hours. She didn't think that her stepmother cared about her safety, but she knew that Ida was most likely furious that Cindy had ruined her plans.

She was also afraid of Ida's magical power, she had no idea what her stepmother was capable of in order to get what she wanted.

"She isn't a very nice person that's for sure, but everything that I've ever owned is in her hands, along with life as I know it," Cindy said, sounding bitter. She hadn't really thought about the consequences when she decided to escape, but now after a good night's sleep she was in turmoil.

Last night she was paralysed, standing on the street alone in the dark. She had no idea what to do. She thought that she'd made some progress the night of the ball, but the fear still paralysed her. She could taste it in the back of her throat as her panic turned into reality.

But then she knew that she needed to find Martha. Cindy forced herself to conquer her weakness and keep going no matter what. She told herself that her fear of stepping into the darkness was silly, and she was a grown woman after all.

Her heart rate was up, sweat rolling down her face, but she continued to walk. She managed to locate the brothel after half an hour. Some drunken peasant finally led her in the right direction. She found Martha at the bar, and as usual the magical hooker was a bit drunk.

Martha's loud burp brought her back to the present. Cindy couldn't believe that she spent a night in the brothel. Luckily, no one had mistaken her for a hooker.

"I need to have a drink before my brain can function properly," she told Cindy, and then pulled out a bottle of vodka from under the bed. "Oh that's a pleasant surprise. I thought I finished this earlier on. Want some?"

"No, thank you," Cindy muttered, feeling a bit nervous. She had to find a way to counter her stepmother's spell and tell the king the truth. Currently Martha had no idea how to help her, and she never heard of that sort of magic.

She watched as Martha took a few generous gulps of vodka and felt a little sick. Today was her wedding day, and she wished that time moved faster. Cindy was very grateful for everything Martha had done for her, but she knew that she couldn't hide in the brothel forever. She was considering seeing Red, but she knew that Ida most likely had already travelled back to Farrington. It was too soon to tell, but Cindy couldn't risk being caught.

"You let that leech get away with treating you like a slave for too long. We need to head to the castle right away," Martha said, and then threw another pretty dress at her. This one was cream and had a small corset around the waist.

"Yes, I need to let Caspian know what she has planned, but I'm sure that my stepmother's spell will prevent me from saying anything at all," Cindy said, and Martha frown like she wanted to agree with germ but instead she said.

"We'll figure something out there and then. I said that I would get you to the ball and I did. Stop worrying about it now and put that dress on. You must look presentable. The king is hot and we need him on our side. If I had been in your position I would have been upfront about Charles and Landis from the very beginning."

Cindy was confused, but she didn't have any other ideas. She knew she would have never met Caspian if it weren't for Martha.

She stripped and changed into the beautiful dress quickly enough. She tossed her old clothes into the bin, put some makeup on, and instantly felt better. Caspian was looking for a wife, and she had to talk to him before he had a chance to meet anyone. She couldn't bear to see him with someone else—she had to stop him and tell him how she truly felt.

Last night all the girls in the brothel were very busy. Despite the reputation of the place, Cindy noticed that the bar was full of men, all looking to pay for sex. She recognised a few from the market, but didn't judge the girls. She had enough on her plate as it was with Ida stupid plan to ruin her reputation by calling her a prostitute.

The girls were thrilled to see her again and they all asked her what happened with the prince once she got to the ball. She took turns telling them about the king and Londis. The girls were sympathetic and told her that she made a good decision to run away.

"Darling, please remember us when you become queen. We would love to visit you some day," Melanie said, and then slapped one of the customers who was attempting to grab her boobs. "Not now, Ricky, you still owe me cash for a blow job from two nights ago."

Cindy giggled, thinking that Melanie was getting a bit ahead of herself. "Queen? I don't think I'm ready for that. I'm only going to the castle to speak to him."

Heat rushed through her body at the thought of seeing him. She missed Caspian and could no longer deny her feelings.

"He's going to fuck her once he sees her. I'm telling ya, they can't keep their hands away from each other," Martha chuckled, appearing by the bar, wearing a black cloak.

"I don't know, he's determined to find a wife. I need to figure this out myself," she told Martha who already looked a little tipsy.

"Maybe you should or maybe you shouldn't," Martha snapped, sounding annoyed that Cindy wasn't listening. "I always thought that Caspian was good looking, and the sex… You shouldn't have run away from the man like that. We'll go to the castle and ask to speak to him. And then once he sees you, he will change his mind right away. From what you've told me, you two have a real connection, right?"

Cindy rolled her eyes, knowing that there was no point in arguing with Martha. The hooker knew better, and she wanted her to be happy again. All the girls wished her good luck and then she and Martha left for the castle. It was midday and Cindy had been up for hours, but all the girls had worked all night, so most of them slept until late. The market was open today, so the roads were much busier than usual. Martha knew a lot of people in town, especially men, but Cindy didn't think that women liked her very much. A lot of them were shooting her infuriating stares when she passed. And one of them even spit in front of her as they both walked by.

"I don't think you're liked very much by the ladies around here," Cindy pointed out when Martha smiled to some older peasant standing by his horse.

"Yes, that's because I've slept with most of those women's husbands, and they can't stand it," she said, and then giggled. "Come on, I want to stop in the tavern first. The barman there owes me a drink."

Cindy should have suspected that Martha wasn't planning to head to the castle straight away. She couldn't argue with her, so she followed her in, wondering how Caspian would react if he saw her now.

The castle could be seen from the distance, and the view made Cindy a little uneasy. She ruined her stepmother's plans, but what if she was too late? Maybe the king was over her being so indecisive. If he only knew that she was under a spell and couldn't tell him the truth, she could make him understand; she just hoped it wasn't too late.

Cindy was surprised that the tavern was filled with customers at this time of day, and almost everyone in there knew Martha. The hooker went up to the bar, smiling and hugging all the men. Cindy stayed behind, not knowing what to do with herself.

"Hey, Cindy, I haven't seen you in ages. Can I buy you a drink?" someone shouted from the other side of the tavern.

Cindy was shocked to see Charles walking up to her and she was even more surprised that he saw her in the tavern. He was smiling and before she knew it he was standing beside her table.

Cindy was confused that he approached her in the first place, after he chose to take Red to the ball instead. Deep down, Cindy hoped that he and Red would get back together. It looked like Martha wasn't going to stop with only one drink, and Cindy wanted to talk to Charles about Red. She thought that the least she could do was try to tell him that he needed to stop messing around with her and finally commit.

"Yes, that would be good," she replied.

Five minutes later, Charles returned with some wine, looking very cheerful. They started talking about the ball and his work for the king. Charles didn't even mention their dates together and it was like he didn't even acknowledge it ever happened. Cindy didn't know what to think, so she sipped her drink, trying to relax a little. Martha was surrounded by men who kept buying her shots. She was laughing and joking with them, and Cindy wondered how long she was planning to stay there.

Charles finally admitted to her that he still loved Red and he wouldn't be able to find a girl like her anywhere else. Cindy smiled, satisfied with the outcome, then got up and went to the restroom, suddenly feeling a little dizzy. The world around her started spinning, but luckily someone caught her before she fell down.

"Don't worry, beautiful, I got you," said a voice that Cindy instantly recognised as Charles. Her limbs were tingling and she felt like she was going to pass out. She wanted to call Martha, but then realised that she couldn't speak.

Seconds later, darkness swallowed her and she drifted off, still thinking about her vampire king.

***

"You want to take away my immortality. What about the fact that I need to feed on humans?" the king asked, thinking about his other vampire abilities. The old witch had saved his life twenty years ago, and now she wanted him to grow old and die.

"I'm taking away what you don't need any more if you want to love this girl. If you won't make a decision now, you will lose her forever," she said, smiling. The king noticed that the old witch was missing her teeth.

"You need to give me proof that you know where she is first," he told her.

"That was necessary," he told himself, realising that he was back in the castle, in his chamber. He shook his head, bringing himself back to the present. What happened with the witch earlier on was unexpected.

"What was that, my lord?" Constant, his advisor, asked, and when the king glanced at him. He should have remembered that he wasn't alone.

He needed to calm down; otherwise he would drive himself crazy. He couldn't change what had already happened. Constant came in to tell him that Jeremy was coming to see him. Apparently, the boy had some news.

"Come closer…come…come and I will show you where she is," he heard the witch's voice in his head again.

He remembered approaching the large pot filled with crystal clear water, smelling blood everywhere, as the craving for Cindy's blood was making him uncomfortable. The witch gestured at him to lean over the pot, and for a second, the king wasn't seeing anything.

Then the water began bubbling and he saw his Cindy. She was carried out of the local tavern by a man who wore the forest ranger uniform. Two girls were waiting for him at the edge of the forest. He smiled at them and they pointed for him to place Cindy in the carriage.

They exchanged some money and then the image started to fade away.

Someone's voice in the chamber reminded him that he needed to focus on the present. He had given the old witch his most precious gift in exchange for Cindy's location and their future together. Time was precious for the king and he didn't want to waste another minute of it waiting around.

"Tell me right away what you found out," he asked Jeremy when he barged into his chamber a second later.

The boy took a few deep breaths and started talking.

"I followed them like you asked me, keeping a safe distance for a little while, and you were right, my lord. Cinderella's stepmother is forcing her into marriage with that Londis farmer. I hid in the bushes and listened to them when they were just about to leave for the Gardland's Kingdom. Cindy's father had left her stepmother Ida in charge of the whole estate, but he put some sort of clause in the will that only gave Ida full ownership in the case of Cindy's death," Jeremy said, pausing for a second to catch his breath. The king thought that the boy had done well to get this information for him. Now Caspian was glad that he went with his gut. Cindy was being forced into marriage. He was angry that she didn't tell him about it when they met at the second ball. "Her stepmother had help, and she managed to track Cindy down a few hours ago. She announced that Cindy is going to be punished for running away. Londis is planning to flog her and Ida approved it, but that's not all. This marriage is just a business transaction for her stepmother. Apparently earlier on she was blackmailing Cindy. She told her if she wouldn't obey her, she would spread the rumour around that Cindy was a hooker, working in the local brothel. The girl was seen with other hookers the night of the first ball and Ida has a witness. I've been hanging around these people all day and heard bits and bobs from her stepsisters too. Ida had someone to create a document that listed Cindy's name on the lease of the brothel. Her stepmother knew that once Cindy reputation was in tatters you wouldn't want to marry her anymore, so she made this story up in order to force her to marry Londis, that way she can legally take over her father's estate with the forged will."

The king clenched his fists, shaking his head as anger flew through his veins. He picked up his cloak, ready to kill someone.

"My lord, my lord, where are—"

"Not now, Constant. I have a wedding to crash. The sooner someone confronts that evil woman the better. It's a complete disgrace," the king roared, already running through the corridors, with Constant right behind him. He shouldn't have wasted his time with the old witch. Now he wasn't even sure if he was going to make it back to Gardland's Kingdom in time to stop that false wedding. It was a few hours ride to the other kingdom. This looked like a set-up from the very beginning. The old witch had given him until sundown to find his love and then he would be a mortal vampire.

He got to the stables and jumped straight away to his white horse. Cindy was unlucky, and her father should have known that Ida couldn't be trusted. That woman only cared about her own interests and she was never planning to tell Cindy the truth.

"My lord...wait, who is that woman?" Constant asked. He was red-faced and holding his chest like he was struggling to keep his balance.

"She's the love of my life. Prepare the castle and pray for me, because I hope that I can get to the other kingdom to stop that damn ceremony."

Chapter Eighteen

Cindy woke up with a really bad headache, panicking because she had no idea where she was. It took her a moment to realise that she was on the move, most likely in a carriage.

Slowly her memories started coming back to her. She recalled heading over to the brothel and asking Martha for help. Then they both went out, leaving for the castle, but they stopped in the tavern and Cindy was chatting with Charles about Red. Then she felt a little dizzy and went to the bathroom. Her memories ended there, and the pain in her head was mounting. She had a feeling that something was terribly wrong.

Then a voice in the darkness startled her.

"Mommy is already planning to punish you for running away. She made a deal with Londis and once you're his wife, he will lock you up in his farm forever."

She recognised Susan's squeaky voice, and noticed that she and Teresa were sitting opposite her. There was also a man in the carriage who looked like a huntsman. He glared at her with his tiny hazel eyes, and Cindy thought he was there to keep an eye on her. Cindy rubbed her eyes and pulled herself to a sitting position. Anger rose within her. She should have known that Ida would send her daughters to find her.

"Your mother can't force me to marry Londis," Cindy snapped, tired of listening to those stupid girls. They weren't her real family, and they had been nothing but cruel to her over the past several years.

Her stepsisters both laughed, then Susan nudged the man with her elbow.

"Oh yes, she can and she will. Mr. Roweling is here to make sure you don't do anything silly. Mommy's sorting out the last bits and bobs for your lame wedding, and welcoming the arriving guests. Londis is paying us good money to take you off our hands," Teresa sang and fluttered her eyelashes towards Mr. Roweling, who totally ignored her.

Cindy noticed that he had a selection of knives by his side, and realised that now she had no chance to sneak away.

"In about two hours everything will be over. Mommy went to the king and he offered to find you, but then we got word that you were in the tavern with some hooker," Susan stated, brushing her red hair. "So we didn't need his help after all."

Cindy glanced out the window, realising that the carriage was moving quite fast. It looked like the coachman was told to hurry up, and she didn't recognise her surroundings. They were probably already halfway to Gardland's Kingdom. Cindy's heart sank in her chest. Ida must have come back to Farrington as soon as she realised that Cindy was missing.

"You can say whatever you want, but I just refuse to stand by him at the altar," she said, folding her hands over her chest and feeling sick.

"We'll see about that," Susan snapped. There was no point discussing anything with them, because her stepsisters weren't listening. Cindy was looking forward to seeing Ida and telling her directly what she thought about her. At the same time she was worried that Ida could force her to say yes to Londis by using her magical powers.

The journey was dragging and her stepsisters were flirting with the huntsman all the way back. She was slowly losing hope, knowing that she had nothing that she could bargain with to change Ida's mind.

If only she had made it to the castle. Caspian would have saved her. Now it was too late for him to do anything. Besides, he didn't even know where she was. Eventually, she drifted off for a bit, hoping that at least Martha was concerned about her safety. The hooker was blessed with magic and Cindy was hoping that she could find a way to stop her wedding.

The carriage stopped an hour later, and the huntsman dragged Cindy out. Ida was already waiting for her outside.

"I underestimated you, Cinderella. I didn't think you had it in you. No one can run away from their responsibilities, not when I'm in charge," Ida stated, staring down at Cindy with her usual stern look. Her stepmother looked relieved, and Cindy's blood pressure rose. "And you will be flogged for almost ruining the wedding."

"I'm not marrying that idiot, Londis. My father wouldn't want that kind of husband for me," she nearly yelled, trying to pull away from the grip of the huntsman, who was hurting her. "You're a rotten human being, and you will pay for this, stepmother!"

Ida shook her head and smoothed her hair.

"Roweland, take her inside the cottage and keep an eye on her. Also, make sure that she puts her wedding dress on. We don't want any more delays. Everyone is already waiting for the ceremony to start," Ida said, through gritted teeth, as if she didn't hear Cindy's insult. "You have embarrassed this family enough, and you will go through with it. I'm sorry, Cindy, but you haven't given me any other choice."

Cindy opened her mouth to tell her that she wasn't done talking to her yet, but Ida was already walking away. The huntsman nearly pierced her skin with his sharp nails when he was dragging her back to the house. She didn't see Londis or anyone else outside. She was taken to a small room upstairs where her ugly wedding dress hang in the wardrobe.

"You have ten minutes to get ready. Don't force me to rip your clothes off and put that dress on you myself," the man said, with a twisted look on his face that made Cindy sick. Luckily, he didn't stay in the room with her, and when he slammed the door behind him, Cindy ran to the window. Her room looked out at the back and that's where she saw that all the guests were already seated. Londis was waiting for her at the altar.

This was her worst nightmare, and she didn't know what to do. She was trapped, but deep down she knew that Ida couldn't force her to say yes to Londis. This was dead simple, and she had already made up her mind. Keeping her reputation wasn't worth ruining her whole life and she could prove Ida was lying, papers or not.

She smiled to herself and quickly put her wedding dress on, knowing that she could still humiliate Ida in front of all the guests if she refused Londis. Her chest felt tight when she tried to breathe.

Her magic could only go so far.

The banging on the door brought her back to reality.

"Well, you look poor and uninteresting. Londis is just going to love it." Teresa giggled with her sister, but Cindy ignored them. She was done listening to their silly insults. She wasn't affected by it anymore.

"Let's just get on with it. I really don't want to waste my time," Cindy barked at them.

She had changed her destiny by running away and she wasn't prepared to give up everything without a fight. Even if that meant she had to scratch Ida's eyes out with her own sharp nails.

She was just looking forward to seeing Ida's face once she said no to Londis at the altar.

"I think Cindy might have lost her mind already. I'm so glad we don't have to deal with her any longer," Susan whispered to Teresa, when she moved past them.

No matter what happened, she had to keep her head held high. People needed to see that she was proud of who she was. Her stepmother wanted to see her tormented and miserable, but Cindy wasn't going to give her the satisfaction.

Her stepmother was outside the house, and she handed Cindy a bucket with yellow flowers without saying a word. It looked like no one was going to walk her down to the altar. Some guests were already turning around. Cindy took a few deep breaths, while her heart was beating frantically in her chest. She was thinking about her late father and Caspian. The king—her king was somewhere out there and as soon as this silly wedding was over, she was planning to head over to the castle.

She started walking, feeling like she was in a fog. The wedding guests were staring at her, and some were even smiling. She thought that she looked terrible. The dress was horrible and not her style at all. On top of everything, she didn't know any of the people who came to celebrate her special day, and it looked like the altar was set right in front of the pigpen. The smell was horrendous and Cindy just couldn't believe this was happening. Over the years, she'd planned her own wedding, imagined every small detail, and in the end, she had ended up here, supposedly marrying a man who made her physically sick.

She approached Londis, who wore a tedious white suit and had a goofy smile plastered across his face. The priest was at least eighty years old and smiled kindly at her, holding a bible in his hands.

"Ladies and gentlemen...we have gathered here today...

She switched off when the priest started talking, trying to think about something else. Cindy was torturing herself, thinking about Caspian and remembering the way he made her feel. A fierce heat built up inside her as she was pumping herself with courage.

She was in love with the vampire king, and even if she wanted to, she couldn't deny it. She wanted to scream at the top of her lungs that she had already found her real love, and that Ida was forcing her to marry the man standing in front of her.

"Now it's time for one of the most important questions of the day." The priest's voice brought her back to the ceremony. Teresa and Susan were giggling away, sitting very close—too close. When she glanced back at Londis, she noticed that he was staring at her boobs.

"Will you, Mark Londis, take this woman, Cinderella Rutherford, to be your lawfully wedded wife, to have and to hold, from this day forward, for better, for worse, for richer, for poorer, in sickness and in health, until death do you part?" the priest asked Londis first.

Cindy's heart was racing away, and her vision went blurry. She couldn't faint now, she still had to humiliate Ida, and let everyone know that she was an evil woman.

Then the question was going to be directed to her. She felt it in her bones.

"I do," Londis answered, smiling at her. Cindy's heart was racing and she thought that his palms were sweaty and disgusting.

Then the priest turned to face her.

"Will you Cinderella Rutherford, take this man, Mark Londis, to be your lawfully wedded husband, to have and to hold, from this day forward, for better, for worse, for richer, for poorer, in sickness and in health, until death do you part?"

Strained silence descended around her, and Cindy couldn't force herself to answer. Everyone was staring at her, and Londis was mouthing in silence "I do" to her, like she had forgotten her vows. Her heart skipped a beat, and she waited…not even knowing for what.

"No, I'm not taking this man as my husband. And you, stepmother can go to hell!" she shouted, shaking with anger.

Then Ida shot back to her feet, going pale and started mouthing something silently. Cindy feared that she was using magic to make Cindy say yes to Londis, but then many of the wedding guests began to turn around again, whispering and Cindy heard a horse jolting from behind them. She noticed someone galloping towards the cottage on a white horse. Her heart stopped, and buzzing started in her ears. She told herself that she was hallucinating again, because she saw dark hair, and a dark cloak as her vampire king tore through the middle of the aisle, then stopped his horse pulling on its reins. Some people screamed, others gasped, and Cindy stood in the same spot, paralysed, when her king jumped off the horse, meeting her eyes.

"Father, stop this whole nonsense. No one is going to force you to marry this clown," Caspian shouted.

"My king, this is a private event," the priest mumbled, looking confused.

"Yes, carry on, Father, please. Cindy is just about to marry the love of—"

"Actually, I just said no…

"Don't even dare say another word, woman. You lied to her, and everyone else out here. You are forcing Cindy into a marriage that she doesn't want with some absurd blackmail," Caspian roared, cutting Ida off, who was already standing up. Cindy placed her hands on her hips and shook her head. Caspian was going to save her either way, but in a way she was a little annoyed that he took the fun of humiliating Ida away from her.

Heat danced on the surface of her skin. She couldn't believe that the king had tracked her down.

Then she glanced at her stepmother, smiling. She wasn't afraid of her magic anymore, besides Cindy officially refused to marry Londis in front of everyone out there.

"Ida forged your father's will and added the clause about the marriage, twisting things around. One of my people has been following her and that clown all day long. He overheard her talking about it, and discussing the final payment she would get for you from Londis. I know about her blackmail and everything else that she has being doing to you over the years." He grabbed her hand and brought her close to his chest.

"I think we've all heard enough," Ida snarled. "Cindy is going to marry Londis, regardless of what you think. My men are here too and they can make sure that Cindy completes her vows." Four other huntsmen stepped in front of her. Cindy didn't see them earlier. Tension tightened across the king's frame and Cindy couldn't believe that Ida was daring to threaten Caspian. Didn't she realise that she was committing a crime?

Maybe her magic wasn't that strong after all.

"Get over here, you stupid girl. We're already practically married!" Londis shouted, trying to grab her, but the king stepped up in front of her and then punched him. The groom went down like a sack of potatoes, falling off the altar. The priest looked bewildered, backing away.

"Are you aware that you're challenging the King of Farrington?" Caspian asked, amusement in his tone. All four men took out their knives and Ida smiled. A few wedding guests were whispering, staring at Ida like she'd gone crazy.

Ida faced him with a vicious smile. "Too bad that you're on your own, my lord. No one should be challenging me, not even the king. Now step away from the girl or my men won't hesitate to kill you."

Chapter Nineteen

The king was amused and in a way impressed that Ida was so determined to win. She was blinded by her greed, and Caspian was planning to teach her a lesson. He squeezed his hand around Cindy's waist as she shivered in his arms.

Four huntsmen moved towards him. The king needed to act fast. He wasn't worried, but at the same time he couldn't expose his supernatural abilities to all the humans standing around. The priest was trying to tell everyone to calm down, while Londis backed away from the altar, his nose and mouth bleeding.

"I'm not losing everything because of you. The estate is mine," Ida snapped, still not backing off.

"You're making a big mistake," Caspian said, a little tired of all the theatrics. Earlier on, he wasn't planning to leave Ida with nothing, but now he decided she didn't deserve his mercy.

"I doubt that. It's you who's making a mistake." She gestured at her men to go ahead and do her dirty work. Caspian was still a vampire, even though his agreement with the old witch took away his immortality. He watched the huntsmen who crept towards him, and then leaned over to Cindy.

"I love you, and I'm sorry that you have to see this," he whispered.

Caspian hated violence, but he wouldn't mind strengthening himself with human blood. Two of them surrounded him and, using his inhuman speed, he took the knife from the smaller one and began slashing their throats, one by one, before any of them realised what was going on. His instinct took over and the beast inside him was awakened. All four huntsmen went down, gasping for breath as the blood poured from their necks. Some guests screamed, others started running away—panic took over the crowd.

The king stood by Ida a half second later, breathing hard. His fangs were out, and he was watching Cindy. He expected to see fear in her eyes, but she looked relieved instead. Londis was mumbling to himself, staring horrified at Ida's men. The priest was asking God to spare him.

Caspian spoke directly into Ida's ear. "I told you that you were making a terrible mistake, but you didn't listen. Now, you're going to pay for all of your lies, my lady. You have not seen me hurting these men. They fought with each other over their lost payment. Once you return to Farrington, my guards will take you away to my prison."

Then he looked at the wedding guests repeating the same thing and using his glamour to make them believe that he'd shown up to rescue Cindy. He changed his mind about feeding on the huntsmen, and partially healed their deep cuts. He didn't want to worry about the mess.

Besides, his Cindy needed to see that he was still a human deep in his heart. Their love could survive anything, and he wanted a clean slate. His glamour drifted around, calming everyone and implanting new memories in their heads. As soon as he took Cindy away, people would believe that the wedding hadn't taken place because the bride had changed her mind.

The huntsmen got up and started arguing, blaming each other for their lost payment.

"What happened? Why are they all so calm?" Cindy asked once his glamour began to take effect on everyone. He didn't want her to stay there a second longer. He had to leave.

"Don't worry, everyone believes that you changed your mind. I'm taking you to Farrington and now you're the sole owner of your father's estate," he said. "Unless of course your stepmother was right and you want to marry Londis?"

Cindy looked like she was still in shock. She glanced at her stepsisters and Ida who were already rushing towards the cottage.

"No, of course not. I really thought that I'd lost you forever," she said, and tears started streaming down her cheeks. The king laughed, and lifted her up, so she couldn't avoid looking at him.

He saw the love in her eyes, and his heart warmed instantly.

"You were very naughty, my Cinderella. You should have told me that your stepmother was blackmailing you. Now, do you want to go back with me to Farrington and at some point become my beloved wife?"

She stared at him with her eyes wide—the king needed to give her some time to gather herself.

"Yes, take me away, I don't want to be here any longer," she pleaded and the king smiled.

He grabbed her hand and lifted her up, so she sat on his horse. Some wedding guests were still watching them; others were leaving. He jumped back on the horse, wrapped his arms around her, and off they went. Caspian whistled, knowing that his life was finally complete—he had his Cinderella back.

***

Cindy was standing in the king's chamber staring down at herself in the huge mirror. Emotions swelled inside her, but she fought back her tears. She couldn't believe that her dreams were finally coming true. She just married the love of her life, the vampire king.

A few months had passed since Caspian rescued her from marrying Londis and Cindy's life had changed dramatically. Her stepmother, Ida, was in prison for treason and fraud.

As soon as she came back to Farrington, the king's guards arrested her. She screamed and shouted as the guards took her away. Caspian told Cindy that Ida didn't deserve any better, and she needed to be taught a harsh lesson.

Cindy felt bad for her, but in a way, she was glad that Ida was being punished. She'd treated her like a slave for years and took advantage of Cindy's good heart and naive nature.

"Do something! Speak to the king and tell him to spare Mommy!" Susan begged her several weeks ago when she arrived back at her father's home.

After everything, Cindy decided that Susan and Teresa should stay in her home, knowing that they had nowhere else to go. Besides, she didn't want to be just like them.

"Prison is the best thing that could have happened to her, Susan. You should be glad, and you should really start thinking about your reputation," she replied. Both of her stepsisters stared at her with fire in their eyes when the king kissed her. They didn't dare insult her again, and Cindy hoped that they started thinking about their actions.

Then a few months later, the king proposed to her during dinner and she agreed without hesitation.

"What are you thinking about, my dear?" a voice that sent a shiver down her spine brought her back to the present.

She needed to stop thinking about the past and just be happy. Londis was left behind at his farm and Cindy was never going to see him again. Even Red couldn't believe that Cindy ended up with the king when she arrived at her home to hand deliver an invitation for the wedding.

Red showed up at the wedding ceremony with another man, ditching the forest ranger once and for all. Later on, she told Cindy that she was taking her future into her own hands too. Cindy still remembered how Charles betrayed her in the tavern, and was silently glad that things turned out this way. She had no idea what happened to him and didn't care one bit.

"I'm thinking that I'm very lucky being here with you—having you in my life," she responded, and Caspian wrapped his strong arms around her. Desire pooled into her stomach and she felt a sweet pulse between her legs. Caspian had been fucking her constantly since their wedding night. They barely left his chamber, but tonight they had another ball. He invited several important guests from other kingdoms to celebrate their marriage once again, and they were already late for the party.

Cindy invited Martha and all the girls from the brothel to the wedding.

"I think I might have a bit of a drinking problem," she admitted to Cindy when a handsome stranger approached her to dance. "But I'll get myself together. Fairy dust always helps."

Cindy was sure that Martha was going to be fine, and she was glad that she tripped over her during that night before the ball. Her life would've turned out so much differently otherwise.

"No, I'm the lucky one, because we can now age together. It isn't an issue anymore. It was all for the best, but I still need blood to survive," Caspian muttered, kissing her neck. She arched her head backwards, thinking that there was something wrong with her hormones. She had a desperate ache between her legs, and she needed to have him again. They had just made love and she even let him drink her blood, pumped with desire. The entire act felt much more erotic and pleasurable than she thought.

"How did we get here?" she asked him, trying to distract herself from lust that continued to build in her system.

She told herself that she needed to stop analysing it for a change. She was finally happy, married to the love of her life, and no one was going to take that away from her.

"Well, I haven't been totally honest with you either, my Cinderella. We met earlier on, before you showed up at the ball that I threw for Eric. I had changed my appearance and became a forest ranger before that night. We met several times and made out in the bushes when your stepmother caught us and dragged you away," the vampire king confessed.

Cindy's jaw dropped. She turned around to face him, remembering all the time she had spent with him believing him to be Charles and exactly what happened that night in the bushes. She'd thought even then that Charles's skin shimmered in the dim light.

"You were Charles all that time? But how?" she asked, staring at the man she loved.

"I needed to feed, so I borrowed his appearance. You stole my heart that day at the market, when you dropped your groceries, so I kept coming back to town, hoping to see you again. I had never felt so alive being with you. I can't explain it any other way," he said and then leaned down to kiss her again. His lips were soft and gentle. The king devoured her like a man starved for intimacy. When he pulled away she was out of breath, but then he started kissing her breasts. She lost her mind when he was around her.

"Yes, I thought there was something different about Charles that day at the market, he was so much more mature and interesting," she muttered, forgetting about the party and wanting to rip Caspian's clothes off. Her throat was a little sore, but she wanted him to bite her again or fuck her—or both. Either way, she needed to feel him between her legs again.

"Let's stay here. I can't stop kissing you and I want to cherish your beautiful body," he rasped into her ear and then pulled her dress down. She giggled and stepped out of it, standing in front of him in her underwear—the same knickers that she left when she ran away after finding out that he was a vampire.

His eyes gleamed and she saw scorching desire that made her even wetter.

"Fuck the ball, I need to have you again, Cindy," the vampire king growled and brought her to his chest. Cindy melted in his arms and thought that this was it. She was in love and happy. She was going to have her happily ever after with the vampire, her own king who would love her forever.

The end

15292015R00118

Printed in Great Britain
by Amazon